THE
AZIZ BEY INCIDENT
AND OTHER STORIES

THE
AZIZ BEY INCIDENT
AND OTHER STORIES

Ayfer Tunç

Translated from the original Turkish by
Stephanie Ateş

English-language edition first published in 2013 by
Istros Books
London, United Kingdom
www.istrosbooks.com

Edited by Feyza Howell and Susan Curtis

Cover image © Anthony Georgieff
Vagabond Media
www.vagabond.bg

ISBN 978-1-908236-11-1

Typeset by Octavo Smith Ltd in Constantia 10/13

This project has been funded with support from the TEDA
Programme of the Ministry of Culture and Tourism of Turkey.

CONTENTS

THE AZIZ BEY INCIDENT

A tragic event occurred at Zeki's tavern one night. Zeki roughed up Aziz Bey and threw him out. No one could quite remember how it began and what happened, but everyone went around making far-fetched claims. Some said, 'Zeki started it'; others objected, 'No, Aziz Bey was as drunk as a skunk.' Some found fault with the patrons, and others said, 'It wasn't worth blowing out of all proportion.'

A few hours after the incident, Aziz Bey went home. He sat for a while in the light of a blinking bulb that settled over the room like a grave illness, and with eyes brimming with tears that just could not fall, he looked at a shattered moonlight reflected in the dirty waters of the Golden Horn and frequently obscured by clouds. The last thing to pass through his mind was the memory of a very short, but very happy time: three days spent in a hot city, blue as far as the eye could see, shaded by palm trees, dates, and other, taller palms. That happiness suddenly changed to sorrow and this was reflected in his face. The sunken old face that had given up hiding the entire suffering of a lifetime full of mistakes seemed for a moment as if about to cry, and stayed that way.

There was no one to softly close his lustreless eyes in the hours that stretched towards the morning of that cold and rainy night. No one to open the fingers crossed over each other like a childishly peevish sign, no one to place his arms as light as a bird on either side. He had slumped into his armchair. The spirit suffering inside him drifted out. He had come to the end of a ruffled life that left a fond memory in very few hearts, and found peace.

It's all over now. The streets stretch out like a giant awakening, and as night falls on the city the locals of those streets still miss him. Gafur the mussel seller asks Boğos the *Agos*-seller[*] about him, Boğos asks Tayfur the lottery agent, and Tayfur asks the hip amputee Ibo, who sells single cigarettes out of the pack. Even Dark Hacı, who sells prayer beads and fragrances on Ağa Mosque Street, looks for him with eyes whose whites are too bright. The locals of those streets miss Aziz Bey – whose secret sorrow they did not sense for years – swaggering down the street in his thread-bare stage costume with purple satin collar and cuffs, carrying his tambur in its faded black case.

The street was orphaned.

Bahri the clarinettist contends what took place that night in Zeki's tavern was a tragic incident. Far better for it not to have happened. Zeki went too far. Of course he was right, but he should not have manhandled Aziz Bey. On the night of the incident, Bahri returned home, lay on his bed and pondered. He didn't know what he thought and why, but he sensed Aziz Bey was different, and that 'such a man never deserved such treatment.' That night sleep escaped him; just as he was about to get up he found what he was looking for: it occurred to him that Aziz Bey was a dusty souvenir of the days when his musician companions counted among respected folk. That's when he ached inside intensely. Bahri is someone who had seen those good old days; he knows the proper way to behave with good manners. He knows very well what loyalty means. If it were not for the memory of those days, he would lose the meaning of life completely.

Mercan the darbuka player, when asked what happened said, 'I didn't see, I don't know, I was in the bog, whatever happened, happened then.' He wasn't in the bog or anything in actual fact, he simply didn't care one way or the other. In fact, he had sort of seen what had happened, but said to himself, 'Who cares?' Mercan doesn't have the soul of a fellow musician. As if the skilful hands

---

[*] The Armenian community's Turkish-language newspaper, est. 1996

8

that beat the darbuka were not his. His mouth may sing, *If the end of this love affair is going to be painful,* but his mind is elsewhere. The day he parks his minibus in front of his door he'll bid farewell to his night-time partners. All he can think of is a blue minibus.

As for Davut the waiter: he saw everything, he knows it all. He'd been secretly anticipating this for days, after all. A nasty piece of work by nature, he's treacherous, venomous, and loves trouble. Even with nothing untoward he says, 'I can feel something bad is going to happen one of these days.' He is innately evil. The one who speaks out of turn most and makes mountains out of molehills all over the place. He laughs with Zeki to his face, and dances attendance on him because he's the boss; but when he feels that Zeki has passed from merrily tipsy to drunk, he fills a bag with bunches of bananas, blocks of cheese, lamb chops by the rack, and takes them straight home.

However much Zeki says about Aziz Bey, 'I was right, I'd had it up to here, that pillock had buggered up the business!' he has grown listless since that night; he looks on the verge of tears. Something inside he can't pin down aches intensely. Some days he thinks it is his stomach that is aching, on others, his heart. He closes the tavern, goes home and sits in front of the window. He looks at the lights sliding like fireflies into the city's night, trying to discern where Aziz Bey's now extinguished light might once have burned, and asks his wife, 'But was I wrong Mukadder?' his eyes brimming, 'Who'd do a thing like that?'

And all his wife replies, unthinkingly, is, 'Oh, for God's sake, Zeki, if I've told you once, I've told you a million times, of course you wuz right,' stretched on the bed, her hair spread out on the pillow, lost in contemplation of the clinking of the gold bangles that cover her right wrist. But no amount of vindication can mollify him; the ache inside does not go away.

As if passing slowly into the sun's shadow, like evening falling unnoticed, Aziz Bey passed from a bright, happy face to a sorrowful one. He acquired a sorrowful past. His nose was always in the

9

air, his head held high. Even if he had not managed to live any other way, he realised that evening, while staring at the dirty waters of the Golden Horn, that in fact he had always made this assumption. Yet he had been gravely mistaken. And again, he realised his life had been nothing but one big misconception.

He went through the streets that resemble no others, where blood-shedding rage and maddening indifference, stone-hard pain and hysterical joy, tragic births and ridiculous deaths, venomous hatred and feeble love, cats and dogs, the crooked and the straight, white and black live together as brothers and sisters of the same parents but tear each other to pieces nevertheless; streets that are too complicated to be understood by those of the respectable life façade, and that resemble a brief summary of the enigma called life. He went, he turned round and came back. His relatively short life was quickly spent on a speck of earth populated by those who fed on one another.

Without knowing all this who could know who was right, and who was wrong?

In actual fact, Aziz Bey should have been seen doing his *tambur taqsim* at the Palace Night Club in his black costume with purple satin collar and cuffs begun by a lachrymose tailor years earlier for a famous stage artist, but left unfinished when he went blind. Aziz Bey used to run from one nightclub to the other; running being a figure of speech. He never ran; more like he could barely keep up with the offers. He swaggered, his nose always in the air, his glance always on the horizon at a lofty point that no one could see. After a great deal of reluctance, he was good enough to oblige with his tambur those waiting patiently to hear his art. Producers would queue at his door during the Izmir Fair. Even if not the most important singers, the next most important ones used to phone Aziz Bey to ask him to back them, and if that didn't work, they would ask through a mediator. He would leave them all waiting at his door. There was a spirit in his playing; his plucking of the tambur was extraordinary. It was like nectar to those who listened. And he'd always been grumpy, too. But he had such a compelling attitude and manner, and a look that said 'I know what I'm doing' that those very capricious singers with painted blue eyelids, teased blonde hair, flirting in sequins, tulle and feathers, swallowed their tongues in his presence.

The truth of the matter is that he never harboured a youthful passion to become a tambur player or anything like that. It was fate that pushed him down this path. At some point in his long and blurred story the tambur stuck to his hand. He was a little flighty, resembling a bird in spirit. He was a dapper lad too and quite handsome. He was constantly falling in love with married women nearing middle age with a penchant for escapades, with broad bosoms and wavy hair. His passion would quickly pass like a soft breeze springing up on summer evenings. Women would send him ridiculous letters wet with tears, written in an uneven scrawl full of clichéd sentences of passion. He would read and then discard them all, laughing as he read them.

He would meet and part from women over and over again under the acacia trees in country tea gardens with wooden chairs. Then? Then nothing... A pack of ladies' cigarettes forgotten on the table was all that remained of almost every woman. After smoking the last cigarette in the forgotten pack, the woman would slip from his mind and disappear. He would not even remember the women he had left without even a backward glance. Those women would look out for his coming, go to the places where they had met and wait for him; they would keep thinking about him and shed tears at night in their beds: did he care? He expected such a passion from life, one that would suddenly hit him like a slap, stupefy him, paralyse him. A love that hit one like that was what Aziz Bey called 'passion'. Becoming a tambur player was the last thing on his mind in those days...

His grandfather used to play a little, in actual fact. Not just a little, he played pretty well. He died before his time, and the tambur became a family keepsake. Aziz Bey's father did not appreciate its value. Not that he'd ever cared to know what it was that permeated its strings. But even so, he didn't have the heart to break and throw away this sole memento of his father; a man who spent his life not being able to say no to anyone, being pushed around, and taking refuge only in the tambur. He put this poor dejected musical instrument away on top of the cupboard.

When he was still just a bleary-eyed child with a runny nose who turned the house upside down, Aziz Bey found the dusty, forgotten tambur where it had been left, on top of the cupboard. After that he never put down this strange toy that was several times taller than himself.

Just for fun, he would keep scraping the bow across the strings. When she heard the tambur's sad tone, his sorrowful mother, usually up to her elbows in water with washing soda, would call to her son in pathetic agitation. 'For goodness sake son, put it back, don't let your father see...' Even though she couldn't cope with a son who wanted to play with the noisy toy all day, the poor woman managed each time to take the tambur away from him and hide it just before his father was due home. When Aziz Bey had grown a little older the tambur quietly passed from his mother and father's room to his own.

Aziz Bey's father was ill tempered; even if there were any delicate feelings chiselled deeply into his soul, he would not let anyone see them. His wife put up with a lot from him. The permanent frown, a fist continually brought down on the table because the food was salty, the shirt not ironed, the bread was stale; the bass voice reproving at every opportunity... But still, at night when all was quiet, when he was boozing on his balcony that almost glimpsed the sea from the slopes of Samatya, his face revealed an unexplained sadness, and he would hum those old, delicate songs that were in his head,

> Who graces your beautiful rose garden
> Who pleads kissing your feet...

Aziz Bey would contend his father hadn't been able marry his true love. Not true. As Aziz Bey had written himself, he had also rewritten his father and his grandfather. There were times when he rewrote a whole lifetime. And he ended up believing it all. After his father was dead and gone, when total loneliness had finally replaced the resentment he felt, he gave his father the benefit of having finer feelings imprisoned in a corner of his heart. In actual fact, his father had married his mother out of love, but was always burdened by life, always struggling to stand upright. Instead of being a downtrodden, submissive child like his extremely sensitive and continually oppressed father, he wanted to be as hard as stone and aloof. That's all there was to it.

As for Aziz Bey, he was a mixture of his grandfather and father; both sensitive and emotional, and yet stubborn and headstrong. And since two proud tightrope walkers tried to walk the same rope, he was in constant strife with his father. His father, a clerk at the courthouse, who shaved even on Sunday mornings and who wouldn't step into the street without a hat, wanted his son to study to be a judge, a prosecutor, or something of the sort, but Aziz Bey was always too frivolous. Dark covered books, frowning teachers, and classrooms with windows painted halfway with grey gloss paint distressed him. Wherever there was a useless, entertaining, fleeting job he went after it. He went on kicking a ball around football pitches until his leg was injured. For a few consecutive years he was a lifeguard at the Florya beach; he liked the appreciative looks of the girls who came to the beach in convertible cars. When he developed a passion for driving, he worked a shared taxi on the Bakırköy-Taksim line. He spent the few piasters he earned at taverns and brothels. Whatever his father did, he did not study; it was his father who gave in first.

But these were teenage years, which always pass so quickly, and so did. His father retired, he began to spend the remainder of his colourless life between home and the coffee house. He suddenly went into decline. He was not able to remember the names of his friends or keep track of things. He owed money everywhere. As he sank into debt his worry and his anger grew. Aziz Bey had just come back from military service; he realised then that fleeting jobs wouldn't earn you a decent crust; one had to hold down a proper job. He was a good-looking lad with a smooth tongue, and his father had a wide circle of friends, so he joined a firm trading in gravel. His mother and father, seeing that he got up early and went to work and returned home in the evening at the right time, began to cultivate hopes that their son would grow up and become responsible. However, this routine did not last for long. As he began to work head down, shoulders stooped saying, 'Yes sir, no sir,' in this gloomy, low-ceilinged office smelling of sweat, tar and onions, with its two small windows looking out onto dark heaps of sand, it began to hit Aziz Bey's day-dreamy head what a hard struggle life really was. On Sunday mornings, when his father was not at home and he tried moaning to his mother, his mother always used to respond, 'Perseverance my son, perseverance...' He certainly was not going to persevere. But it went against the grain to ask for pocket money from his aloof, obstinate, white-haired father. Even if he didn't persevere he worked patiently through the day, longing impatiently for the evenings.

It was at that time he began to frequent the taverns that opened wide the windows of his expansive soul, and that thrilled his insides as he touched the strings of his musical instrument. He was still on bad terms with his father. They did not even have dinner together any more. As soon as Aziz Bey left work he'd go to the tavern where his tambur would be waiting for him, have a table set with *rakı* and *meze* and would sing, accompanying his older musician friends,

> Even if you pale and fade you are still a rose-pink mouth
> If God should have a blessing for me that's you.

He'd smile thinking of Maryam, convinced by now she was standing and waiting by the window as he passed her door every morning, and believing that he'd found the love he was looking for, since every glimpse of her shook him as if he had been slapped.

*

Aziz Bey's tragedy begins with Maryam: simply because he fell in love with her. This love like a blind eye, a paralysed right arm, a heart missing a beat, always gave him pain but lived on with him.

It would have been all right if only he had been able to think of Maryam as one of those broad-bosomed, teary-eyed women on the list he kept when he was a teenager. It would have been all right if it were just a sexual desire that had stirred inside him, if he had looked at Maryam's body as fresh as a sapling hastening to grow, as a very thirsty person looks at a frosty glass of water, if he had just been content to desire that body. But Aziz Bey looked into Maryam's eyes. That eyes were dangerous, he understood only after Maryam. If he had not kept thinking about her eyes that spoke, if he had not flushed to the tips of his toes when he saw her, if his knees had not shaken, his tongue had not stuck to the roof of his mouth, Aziz Bey would have been a man like everyone else.

What would have happened if he had been a man like everyone else? Nothing... But perhaps he would have lived longer. Perhaps he would have aged by rotting gradually, become bent and would have forgotten the song, *Months pass and I'm still waiting for you to come.* He would have married a woman who talked incessantly and grew fatter by the day. He would have left that semblance of an office and joined a largeish firm. He would have earned more money, each month he would have got hold of pen and paper and drawn up long accounts and each time decided to give up smoking. He would have had twin boys whose heads he would have clipped for always breaking windows playing ball, and whom he would have wanted to study to be a prosecutor or a judge, or perhaps he would have had a girl. He would then learn that his daughter had slept with all the young lads in the neighbourhood, and this would have caused him great anguish. However, he would have been so entangled with life that he would pretend he didn't know. Feigning ignorance would not offend him; he would not question why it had not offended.

If it had not been for that touching thing he thought he had caught in Maryam's eyes, that dripped like a bitter draught into his heart, Aziz Bey would have died one day slumped over a steel desk with a sheet of glass cut for the top, filling in the same old ledgers, because life would have ordered him to work on, even though he should have retired long ago

And so he would have lived a life like everyone else.

But that's not what happened. After Maryam. Aziz Bey, who was spoiled by the appreciation of women whom he scorned, was transfixed one day by Maryam's black eyes, deep as a well, looking out from behind a net curtain. 'I was as good as bewitched' was how he described that unforgettable moment to those who at the time he was very close to, most of whom are now no longer alive. It was as though what he experienced at that moment was not love but a divine call. What he saw was not a pair of eyes but the first sign of a strange destiny calling him to a warm but dark and mysterious world. That this world was poisonous, he realised much later.

And yet, it's impossible to rule out the role fate in his story. If he had not worked in that office, if the way to the office had not passed in front of Maryam's house, if Maryam's family had not lived on the ground floor of that shabby apartment, if that pair of well-like eyes that he had fallen in love with had not been at home all day sitting in front of the window (she had left work because her boss had gone bankrupt), none of this would have befallen him.

But what had befallen him? It was just a love gone wrong; that is all. Whose life doesn't contain an unhappy love story? However, Aziz Bey's unhappy love story permeated his whole life like a road of no return, an illness that somehow never got better. As Aziz Bey tried to catch the mistake, he walked towards the mistake as though walking towards a yellow leaf that the wind continually blew in front of him, he just could not catch it.

Whenever he thought about Maryam he felt a sweet coolness on his tongue. A feeling tasting of peppermint roamed inside him.

Then a long lasting bitterness would take its place. He always avoided remembering the time preceding this love, the moments of indecisiveness whether or not to begin, those most delectable moments, the dreamiest stage. In fact he was right to want to forget. As he remembered, he remembered how his life had changed its course and how he had been crushed under the load of a weighty misconception.

Furthermore, in the beginning theirs too was a love like everyone else's. But fate obstructed it from progressing like everyone else's. From chance meetings, ostensibly returning from the market as he left work; bashful smiles as their eyes met; the dropping of notes with meeting places written on them; they progressed to brief meetings out of sight that in time became longer. Kissing, making love... Cinemas were visited, boxes reserved; there was swimming at Kilyos; caramelised milk puddings eaten at pudding shops with marble tables. The house was left with little lies. Loitering in vain in front of post offices when the other couldn't leave the house...

It would have been all right if it had carried on like this.

If Maryam's family had not decided to go to Beirut in search of a living, this everyday love would have stretched like chewing gum and perished; what with moods, jealousies and quarrels, it would have run its course and each of them would have put it down to a youthful passion. An Aziz Bey crossed in love would have caused trouble in the taverns, gone round wreaking havoc, philandered a little longer, settled down with time and would have married a suitable girl that his mother would have found for him. The same would go for Maryam. She probably would have married a clumsy, ineffectual, cowardly shoe-seller or meze cook, who first checked his safe as soon as he opened his shop and who dozed on the sofa at night. She would have had a summerhouse on the Islands. On starry, hot summer nights she would not be able to sleep for thinking about Aziz Bey, his body full of life. Maryam would very likely be richer and would not even live in the same district as Aziz Bey. Perhaps Maryam would catch a glimpse of him while out shopping one day and be made giddy by her old love, she would walk around her house for a while like a zombie...

Anyway... That's not what happened. Maryam came from a poor family. Her uncle Artin, a furrier, had settled in Beirut a while before. Maryam did not know that her father and uncle had been corresponding for some time and that her uncle insistently summoned her father to Beirut, to be his dependable assistant in this foreign land. One Sunday evening, her father announced his decision. They were not getting anywhere in this country. He was fed up of working himself to the bone. That is why the whole family was to go to Beirut and share in uncle Artin's work. Although that night Maryam cried until the morning thinking of Aziz Bey, she was quickly seduced by the postcards, photographs, the smartness of her cousins and the happy smiles that came from Beirut during the week following this decision.

Maryam used to say, 'It will only be a few months before we come back, my father won't be able to cope there.' She convinced Aziz Bey too. She indicated a vague departure date – today or tomorrow – but never a precise day and time, making it obvious she did not want to say goodbye.

One morning, when Aziz Bey least expected it, as he was going to the office, a horse and cart suddenly appeared in front of him in the street where Maryam lived. Goods sold to the rag and bone man were being loaded onto the cart. He took shelter in the shade of an apartment at the top end of the street and watched the armchairs, coffee tables, thin mattresses, quilts, tinned copper pans, samovar, and even old coats and winter boots being loaded onto the cart. His eyes brimmed with tears. Without moving, he watched the commotion of this family, a member of which was also the girl he loved, preparing to leave for a new country. Then Maryam, her mother, father and sister, hands akimbo, glanced at their home from outside, and loaded a few shabby old cases, tied tightly with washing line, into a chequered taxi. Waving to their neighbours, they got into the taxi with smiling, hopeful faces and departed.

That day Aziz Bey was hurt for the first time. Even if Maryam had not told him about her departure, he thought she would have been sad, tearful and reluctant; she would have turned and gone into the house a few times. In the image of departure he visualised, Maryam would sit, crying in front of the front door, her mother tugging her up by the arms, her father kicking the taxi's wheels and shaking his index finger furiously at Maryam, while her mother stepped in front of her husband in order to stop him beating her, while her sister whispered in her ear, begging. Maryam should not have been able to get up and go at all, as she gazed towards the end of the street, looking for Aziz Bey.

That's not what happened. Maryam, like the others, bustled in and out of the apartment, carried belongings, and never once turned her head to look towards the end of the street. Had she looked she would have seen Aziz Bey's eyes filled with tears, his hurt, unhappy, besotted state.

Ruling out events such as his quarrels with his father and his grandfather's death, this departure was the first disaster in Aziz Bey's life. The subsequent tragic events were added to this first large ring and thus Aziz Bey's life became a very long chain woven from sad times. The good and happy days in the interim were not able to change this melancholy mood one little bit. Whenever Aziz Bey looked back on his life he saw that all that was left from all those years that had been lived, were just a few melancholy and fractured stories.

If that departure, which felt like a nail being separated from his flesh, had not taken place, this love would not really have been love. Aziz Bey went crazy with love; he was too young. He thought that there could never be a greater torment than this and that he would end up dying in the streets deliriously calling Maryam's name. However, he did not know that there are very few moments when the body does not betray the soul: no matter how much one would love to waste away and die after great grief, one cannot succeed. The soul struggles to rise to the heavens donning a black halo but the body is worldly; it eats, drinks and lives.

Aziz Bey did not die; he could not die, but he was no longer able to notice the looks of mature women who enjoyed escapades, hooked on his dark and sharp features; he could no longer read the desire in their trembling nostrils. He lost weight; he grew pale. While his mother feared that he would contract tuberculosis, his father knew, as did the whole neighbourhood, and was proud of the mass of love affairs. He thought that this too was a passing affair of the heart and did not take any notice, saying simply, 'such things happened to me too, he'll recover,' and thereby reminding his wife of his former lovers and probably breaking her heart for the umpteenth time.

After this departure, Aziz Bey began to think that it was not worth believing in love and falling under its power. Just as he had decided to be more ruthless towards women, a long letter arrived from Maryam. It was sincere, touching and extremely romantic. All Aziz Bey's views on love changed in a trice. Man needs to love someone, and to love passionately.

He began to write long and poetic letters to Maryam. His writing was atrocious; even he had difficulty in reading it. Every morning when he arrived at the office he looked with envy at the writing of the accountant filling unnecessary ledgers with beautiful letters; even though he thought about getting him to make a fair copy of these long and extremely private letters, he was too embarrassed to suggest it. So it took him several nights to write a letter. While the light in his room shone, his father muttered angrily remembering the electricity bills and grumbling in a loud voice, 'If you'd had your light on that much when you went to school, you'd have become a somebody by now.'

Just as Aziz Bey feared that being so far out of sight would also be reflected in Maryam's mind, he would receive a new letter; and strangely enough, those letters arriving from a hot and distant city did not become less frequent or shorter.

However, if Aziz Bey had paid a little more attention he would have been able to see in the answering letters, written on wafer thin pink paper with painstaking writing slanting to the left with the tails of the y's rounded and tiny circles dotting the i's, that these letters were based not on love but on an insatiable curiosity for what was left behind. If someone not in love read these clichéd lines taken from films and novels, he or she would have easily realised that Maryam was one of those women who took pleasure not in love itself, but in the devastation it left behind. But Aziz Bey did not understand this at all. In fact he was not altogether to blame. Just as Maryam was one of those women who took pleasure from the ruined lover she left behind, so Aziz Bey was one of those men who believed that there was no woman who would not fall in love with him. The countless women who had entered his life since his youth were the reason for his self-confidence. Of course it was impossible for Aziz Bey's distant sweetheart to forget him.

Maryam's letters always begun with the words, 'your days spent without me...' and were full of questions passionately picking at the sincere feelings of the lover she left behind. Yet there was the air of an experienced mature woman rather than that of a young girl who was forced to go far away and who was impassioned by a childish love. This sweetheart whom Aziz Bey imagined biting the top of her pen while writing letters full of innocent and inquiring questions, described in the same long letters everything about her new home, its magnificence and beauty; she wrote that even though it was very beautiful, they were, in this country as hot as hell, only able to breathe at night, that their situation was rapidly improving, and she invited Aziz Bey to this new prosperous country with very sincere sentences whose reality had not been tested.

'You come too,' said Maryam. 'Without you, days drag on...'

As Aziz Bey received this heartfelt invitation he trembled, little realising these sentences looked good only on paper.

*

And so it was these invitations, written on pink paper that seduced him.

The expected happened at the end of a day when he was lost in thought over Maryam's letters and postcards; he was fired. Hearing this, his father kicked him out of the house in order to knock some sense into this son whose lovelorn state had lost its charm. Actually, his intention was to leave Aziz Bey outside long enough to learn his lesson and so teach by experience just what life was all about. His own father had failed to do that, leaving his son lost in a moderate and harmonious world: and hadn't that been the best thing to do? If he had been more of a disciplinarian, taken an interest in everything, in his son and daughter, if he had forced them to study, to grow into responsible people, would he have spent his life going to and fro between a run-down house and a run-down bureau?

The idea and the deed meant well was naïve. But what his father couldn't have predicted was where it would lead.

His father was sitting in the coffee house playing rummy when, with still two hours until the end of the workday, Aziz Bey went sauntering past. He was still dressed up to the nines, but despite his neat and pressed clothes, there was something dishevelled in his manner and air, something flighty. He had taken off his tie and put it in his pocket. In this state that handsome youth looked like an idle child who had skipped school. He walked rolling a stone over and over with his foot as if life were just a carefree, light-hearted, merry game; he looked as though he couldn't care less about what happened tomorrow.

His father grasped it at once. It was obvious that this was going to happen. He paled and his lips trembled. He asked the coffee house owner for a glass of water. He sipped the water down. Despite his plight he sat in the coffee house until evening, abandoned the game he was playing and thought about his son who, although a fully-grown man, was still frivolous; and this made him grow angry. He returned home at his usual time to find his son lying on the couch reading a newspaper and not looking particularly upset at being fired. He was taken aback.

He imagined that his son would stand in front of him at least a bit crestfallen, looking troubled, and find some excuse, however feeble, for being fired. He gave a little cough, bent his head and found an unaccustomed tone for his voice. He sat in his armchair in a way that was neither as harsh as usual nor as mild as not to be expected of him.

'Why did you come home from work early?' he asked.

Aziz Bey shook his shoulders indifferently while turning the page of the newspaper he was reading.

'I was fired...' he said.

This statement, that issued from Aziz Bey's mouth calmly and naturally as though it were the most normal thing, immediately strained the atmosphere in the house. His father drew a deep breath and began to speak, growing angrier, with his voice rending as his anger grew. He said whatever came to his mind, whatever was on his tongue. As he shouted sentences full of insult at Aziz Bey, his mother became more anguished and looked from her son to her husband as if tongue-tied. There was an indescribable sadness in her face. At every biting word she shuddered as if she'd been punched, and shut her eyes tightly.

Aziz Bey was branded a rogue, a beggar and a good-for-nothing. Insulting sentences verging on curses reverberated round the walls of the room; yet a joy as light as an egg white that froths the more it is whisked, unexpectedly began to form inside Aziz Bey. The father, unaware of the letters calling his son to a hot country scented with a mingling of smells of spices, flowers and lemon, finally booted him out of the house. He told him that he was only fit for common brothels and the filthy streets.

'Don't stand there any longer soiling this decent and honourable house!' he said, 'Get lost!...'

At that point, his mother had covered her face with her hands. Aziz Bey quickly left the room and went to his own room. He filled the case that he had put on his bed and had looked at for days but somehow had not had the courage to fill, he, took his tambur and left. He had intended to say goodbye to his mother, but at the door he met his father.

'Are you still here?' said his father. 'Haven't you fucked off yet?'

Tears sprang to Aziz Bey's eyes and he flushed. He looked at his father bitterly, and slammed the door with such force that the glass decorated with ironwork in a tulip design fell out with a crash. At that point, his mother, whose heart had been beating abnormally fast since the beginning of the quarrel, collapsed on the floor, no longer able to stand the burden of this disaster.

Aziz Bey, not even considering what he had left behind, was ready to embark, full of desire and strength, Brandon a journey to a new home where his sweetheart awaited. As he left the house with rapid steps, he could feel his father's eyes boring into the back of his head. It was as though he feared that his father would seize him by the shoulder with his strong fingers and bring him back to that deadly captivity, just when he was hurrying to reach the freedom he sought in faraway places and leave behind this neighbourhood, where he had been born and had grown up. As he went to the port seeking a ship to take him to a new life promising him riches, love and happiness, his father had taken his ailing mother in his arms, helped her into a taxi and was trying to reach the hospital in time, swearing on the way that he would never forgive his only and ungrateful son, and filled with a resentment so deeply rooted that it would never ever be eradicated.

There were ships in the port that day, but that the one destined for Aziz Bey was still waiting to weigh anchor twenty days later. After Maryam had written, 'You, too, should come...' he had secretly obtained a passport and inquired into travel by train and boat. As soon as he left home, his first job was to go to the port and stare hungrily at the ships that were to take him to his new homeland.

For twenty days, he slept in different people's houses, stayed up all night in his regular taverns and killed time in the coffee houses. He avoided his own neighbourhood throughout. He went round to see his friends, said goodbye, telling them about his wonderful dreams as though they would surely materialise. Because his wasteful palms did not know how to hang on to money, he had not saved the necessary funds for his journey. He borrowed from here and there. He did not even call on his beloved aunt lest she try to reconcile him with his father. He talked to manning agents who recruited seamen and finally boarded a dry goods ship on the condition that he worked his passage.

As he recalled the image of his mother whom he had left behind, he waved his hand like chasing away flies; he wanted to drive away this image that wrenched his insides. Finally he reached the blue and white city so bright it dazzled the eye, far hotter than described in Maryam's letters.

Those three happy days that he happened to be thinking about, sitting in front of the window looking at the moonlight reflected in the Golden Horn on the night of that tragic incident, constituted just a short fragment of this long period.

During the daytime, he did the heavy work shown to him by the expressionless seamen who were as hard as stone with skins leathered by a windy heat. At night, he played the tambur to allay the longing a little. Then he lay on the tarpaulin on the deck of the ship that rocked like a cradle over the foaming waters of the moonlight Mediterranean, thinking of the moment when he would meet Maryam again. What would Maryam be doing? What would she say when she saw him? Would she be at a loss for words? Would she jump into his arms for joy?

Sadly, he realised much later that he had thought about all this for nights on end in vain. Because the first moment of that meeting with Maryam who, as she had related in her letters, was working as an assistant in her uncle Artin's shop, was extremely subdued, passionless, and even cold.

Yet neither was culpable for the cold and emotionless nature of that reunion both had so longed for. For a start, Maryam had written 'come!' on wafer-thin pink paper only after lying in her bed towards morning, exhausted from dealing with furs that burnt her arms and legs like pepper all day long in the city scorched by the sun. She had never considered that Aziz Bey really would be able to get up and come, and harboured a notion that this love, whose existence she found very romantic, would remain a childish poetic game played with letters.

That was the reason she had not been able to believe her eyes when she first saw Aziz Bey, who was thoroughly burnt by the sun while washing the decks during the journey and was in a pitiful and downtrodden state brought about by being in a strange country with no knowledge of the language or place. Furthermore, in place of the strong, protective, decisive young man she knew as Aziz Bey, rough even in his love, here was a poor creature, bewildered and lost like a puppy thrown out of home.

As for Aziz Bey; he was unaware of his distraught and timid demeanour. He had, however, kept his self confident, dignified bearing until the vessel docked; he had held his head high with frequent thoughts of Maryam. During the journey he had such a persuasive manner convincing those around him that he had a strong personality, that he had even impressed the sailors who had turned to stone from being all alone on the open sea. These steely-eyed, sharp-featured and callous sailors, who looked on the verge of cutting one another's throats, could not refrain from swallowing before they ordered him to task.

But this proud manner that had permeated Aziz Bey's body, his looks, and his bearing vanished in a trice in front of the fatal feeling of foreignness he experienced as soon as he put foot on land. His shoulders drooped and an inexplicable timidity settled in his eyes. He was rendered totally wretched by a deep regret when faced with the police who pushed and shoved him, speaking with strange, misty words and loud voices and looking at great length first at his passport and then his face.. When he left Customs and held out the paper with the address to find Maryam to the taxi driver, he was really frightened of the days that awaited him. That was the reason Maryam was confronted not by an Aziz Bey whose look defiantly at the world, but by a crestfallen Aziz Bey ready to bow to any game fate would play with him.

Thank goodness this cool, subdued and strange moment of reencounter did not last very long.

Would it have been better for Aziz Bey if it had lasted? If it had happened in a different way: if Maryam had given Aziz Bey the cold shoulder, if she had said, 'Just because I said come, it didn't have to be at once,' would Aziz Bey have gone straight back? Who knows? And then, what kind of Aziz Bey would have lived in the streets of Istanbul, it is not possible to predict.

And that's not how it happened. After a few pointless questions, asked through her confusion, she realised that she had a lover passionate enough to leave his country for her, and the soft and happy expression given to her face by this treasure lasted a whole three days.

Luckily at that time they were alone in the shop. Maryam's father, uncle and cousins were all in the workshop. And it was lunchtime to boot. As the childish surprise on Aziz Bey's face began to fade, Maryam looked around her. It was as though the city had melted under the heat, people had fled to shady corners like insects. Maryam, seeing no one about, embraced her passionate and faithful lover and kissed him on lips that were dried and cracked by the sun.

And it was this that destroyed Aziz Bey.

That passionate kiss they enjoyed the first day in the lunch break in the dim shop subsequently came as a big shock to Aziz Bey. He was not able to explain to himself how the girl who kissed him so passionately and who went around drunk with love for three days could change so much in one day. It was quite simple, however. For Maryam the only important thing was the existence of such a lover. It was not important whether it was Aziz Bey or someone else. So because Aziz Bey would never be willing to accept this explanation, he never even considered its validity. He looked for other reasons and he could not find any.

After looking long and deeply into Maryam's black eyes that he had missed so much, after caressing her slim white neck, they left the shop, Maryam in front and Aziz Bey behind. Although it was well after midday the sun was too hot to bear; Aziz Bey thought he would go blind from so much light. The paradise he dreamed of was much hotter than he expected and very alien too. Maryam led him round a whole lot of streets: some narrow, some wide, some shady, and some strong smelling, their colours intermingled and cloudy, then decomposing again; hoarse voices, whispers, calls, bursts of laughter, blended with interjections; where huge moustached men slept snoring in the shade. When she finished the journey, they were in front of a small, mean hotel. Speaking in the broken words of a misty language, she took the key to Aziz Bey's room and with confident steps took him upstairs, as though she knew the way. The room was so hot that Aziz Bey thought the walls would melt and run. Maryam closed the shutters of this small, dirty room, and the sweet gloom that enveloped the inside stopped the pain in Aziz Bey's eyes.

Maryam came to the hotel every lunch break over those unforgettable three days that remained engraved in Aziz Bey's mind. The image of the passion they enjoyed in the space of time so much longer than a long lunch break still seemed very short to Aziz Bey as the details were seared into his mind. His whole life was spent striving to tear, eradicate, scrape that image from his brain; he did not succeed. He was never able to remove this error from his being. For this reason, he lived an unhappy and irritable life; mostly angry, but sometimes as aggrieved as a motherless child.

Aziz Bey always believed he had been deceived by Maryam. Yet, if one discounted the sincere appeals in Maryam's letters, one could hardly describe what he experienced as deception. In truth, Aziz Bey had fallen into the mistake of believing he was loved. This was all.

He spent the Maryam-less hours of these three days scarcely able to contain himself, waiting for her to come. On the fourth day, Maryam did not come. Aziz Bey was frantic. He wandered along the corridors of the hotel, he sat in the lobby, he went outside the front door. Lunch break ended, the sun bowed down; as much of the evening he could see from the window of his room slowly descended upon the city, turning it from purple to navy blue. The city metamorphosed, became alive. It became colourful with the lights that filtered through the darkness. But Aziz Bey was not even aware of this. Although he had eaten nothing all day long he did not feel hungry. There was a pain bigger than hunger inside him. As he burnt with the heat, he soaked a white towel turned purple from over-washing and placed it on the nape of his neck, he tossed and turned on the bed. He could not sleep until the morning. He spent the night watching the insects wandering about the creaking floorboards of the hotel room and jumping up with a start at the sound of every footstep. He went out with the first light of the morning passing in front of the young hotel clerk, who leant back asleep in his chair, his mouth open and his face and eyes covered with flies that were landing and taking off. He squatted on the ground and gazed at the road for a long time.

That day during lunch break Maryam stopped by for five minutes. She was coolish, apparently indifferent. She had no intention of asking after Aziz Bey, nor of talking about the job they would find for him, their fresh hopes and wonderful dreams.

To Aziz Bey's 'Why didn't you come yesterday?' she just said, 'I was busy in the workshop, I couldn't leave.' Aziz Bey could not tell her how he worried about her, how he felt like a blind person not knowing the language or his way around this city. He only managed to kiss the edge of her lip, just touch her curly black hair. That was all. When Maryam left, he lay down on his bed, and a stupid smile spread over his face. If only for five minutes Maryam had come, hadn't she? He was happy.

But on the next day she did not come.

That day Aziz Bey had a feeling that there was something funny going on. Something very slender broke inside him. He sat in front of the window, whose shutters he had closed. Hours passed. When one panel of the shutters opened by itself, he saw that the fallen stars of lights from the city had filtered into a sky wrapped in a dark navy blue. He felt as though he had awoken from a long dream. He wiped his tear filled eyes, calmed himself down and walked around the room. A touching expression of acceptance of fate settled on his face. At that moment, he felt completely alone in the world, forlorn and forgotten.

He longed passionately for his mother's sagging soft white neck. If he had been in Istanbul now and been able to bury his face in his mother's warm, white neck, his sorrow could have been somewhat abated.

While looking at the bright lights of this terribly hot city, he remembered that it was time for the musical show at the tavern in Samatya that he visited every evening. The friendly group of musicians must have already come in, one by one, taken their positions, and drunk their first sips of rakı. He thought that they would start a little later with a violin or lute improvisation and that they would soon be lost in a world of their own by giving their souls up to the music that had permeated their cells. He took the tambur that he had not taken in his hand since the day he arrived out of its cover and began to play.

> Black eyes do not heed my wails
> Come oh dimple, come to the rescue...

He put down the tambur and cried his heart out and then felt better. He went and washed his hands and face with this hot city's water that didn't know how to be cool. He sat on the bed and counted the remainder of his money. He then went out, without straying too far from the hotel, went into a shop and ate a tomato salad with hummus and drank a Turkish coffee with cardamom. For a while he wandered around the streets whose sounds and smells had changed with the coming of night, then returned to his room. He was tearful. He was hurt. He felt he had been deceived. He wanted to sleep for a long time and when he woke up find himself in Istanbul as the young Aziz who had not as yet been dealt life's blow. To see that all he had been through had been a bad dream... But no. That harsh reality was real. He was alone and helpless in a foreign land.

Aziz Bey would fall into a similar situation once again at the end of his life. Then too he wanted to go to sleep and when he awoke see that that tormenting phase of his life had never happened. Like so many people whose lives were stamped with regrets...

He lay on his bed. But it was too hot to sleep.

When Maryam did not come the next day or the day after, he was charitably concerned that maybe something had happened to her. If that were not the case, Maryam would certainly have come. He went to the furrier shop of Maryam's uncle, Artin, risking getting lost in those muddled streets. He had a bad feeling inside. He thought he would find the shop closed. The shop would surely be in a cheerless, sorrowful state: the shutters rolled down, the lights off, as if everyone had gone off in a hurry...

But the shop was open and cheerful. It looked as though it were participating with all its inner being in a commercial life full of hustle and bustle. He drew near to the shop, stood in the doorway and looked inside. Maryam was not there. Instead, a thin bony man with a moustache that resembled a toothbrush dipped in black ink, and a fat youth whose drenched handkerchief lay on the nape of his sweaty neck, were talking and looking at a fur coat they had spread on the counter. He listened to them carefully. When he distinguished 'Artin' a few times among the Arabic words spoken in a booming voice by the boy, he realised that the man with the toothbrush moustache was her Artin. For a moment he thought about going in and asking about Maryam, but as uncle Artin turned, sensing someone standing in the doorway, he quickly drew away from the door of the shop as if caught red-handed and crouched at the bottom of a wall. It was as though his heart beat in his throat. He went to the corner of the shop window and looked in. Being the summer season there was just a short jacket made of fox fur dyed blue in the window. Aziz Bey could see uncle Artin laughing cheerfully from behind that jacket. There was nothing untoward. But then, there was no Maryam either.

Although he had tried very hard to remember the way back to his hotel, he got lost in the muddled streets of this city that looked both very like, and not at all like, his own city. His temples throbbed. He felt desperately tired. The deep pain inside him confused his poor mind and slowed his steps as it tried to find the street that led to his hotel. He was so paralysed by the vast variety of words he heard, not a single one of which he understood, that he could not even stop someone and tell him the name of his hotel. He went in and out of many streets. He passed through districts bearing different souls of the city. After finding himself in tiny completely unexpected squares and after drinking water cupping his hand to a street fountain, he finally reached his hotel bathed in sweat, when the redness of the sun had already covered the sky. He paused as he passed the clerk, who was engaged in combing his wispy moustache in a hand-held mirror. He looked hopefully at his face wondering if he would slip him a note, a chit, give him news that would in an instant wipe out all his sorrow. The clerk just smiled. He went up to his room, washed his hands and face and sank down onto his bed. He did not want to believe that Maryam would not come again; he went to sleep.

He waited at the hotel for Maryam for a whole eleven days, hoping she would come. Twice a day he went to the restaurant he had got to know and had a bite to eat. Every morning he went down to the bench that could be called the reception and paid the clerk the money for the night he had stayed. He sat in a corner looking onto the street in front of the so-called lobby and at night played his tambur in his room. The agony of foreignness that had left deep scars on his life took the place of the agony of love. Finally his money ran out.

Words full of bitterness and rebellion were growing inside him. He could neither stay nor return. If he wrote a letter to his father or close friends asking for money, by the time it arrived he would have died of hunger. He felt very deeply the pain of having come to this city with great hopes where he knew no one and where he had not a single friend, only to be disappointed. He wandered around the city for a few days, but he didn't even know the two or three words necessary to be able to get a job. He passed in front of building sites, not being able to explain that he would carry stones if need be, looking with a vacant expression at the workers running about like ants, then returning to his room, hopeless and despondent. Soon he would not be able to pay for the hotel and the clerk who liked to accompany the cheerful songs on the radio would seize him by the collar and sling him out.

That day he wandered around the city yet again and returned to the hotel with his hands empty. It was getting towards evening. Again that beautiful redness had settled on the city. There was no one in the hotel where only vagrants and lonely people stayed for a few days and then left, whose corridors were always empty, where occasionally a cry or a strange shout rose and died away. Despite the fact that Aziz Bey had opened the windows and the door wide, not even the slightest breeze could be felt. He took his tambur and sat on his bed. His woeful voice wandered round the corridors of the empty hotel, reaching even the ear of the young clerk, who was sitting leant back in his chair as usual.

My heart, the day has ended again with separation; the sun has set. Shame, hope has deceived you yet another day, my heart...

The clerk was drawn towards this music, whose words he did not understand but which quietly penetrated his heart. To be able to hear better, he went upstairs and put his head round the door of Aziz Bey's room. There was reverence and wonder on his face, but Aziz Bey who was lost in the melodies of his own music did not even notice it. The song ended and when Aziz Bey lifted his head he saw the clerk in front of him, looking at him with a broken smile. Knowing full well that the clerk did not understand, he said, 'That's how it is mister clerk. Look, hope has deceived me yet another day.'

All he ate that night was bread.

The next day he felt weak and spent the whole day in bed, turning first one way then the other. Towards the evening he got up and, looking at his growth of beard in the mirror whose silvering had flaked off, he thought how he must first find someone who understood his language. Wasn't there a consulate or something in this city? At that point the clerk came. He was speaking continuously in the city's complicated and misty language, but in a really noisy and excited way, as if trying to tell Aziz Bey something. He pointed to the tambur lying on the bed. Aziz Bey smiled, he thought the clerk wanted a song, took the tambur and sat on the bed. However, the clerk took Aziz Bey by the arm, showed him his clothes and succeeded in explaining to him with weird movements that he wanted him to follow him.

Aziz Bey got dressed in a state of bewilderment, took his tambur and followed the clerk. Dusk had fallen. It was as though the people of the city who could not go out during the day because of the heat had now flowed onto the streets and they were full of lights, alive. There was a delicately sweet fragrance in the still hot air. It was as if a sharp scent of jasmine pervaded the air from somewhere and in a funny way also gave Aziz Bey the will to live. This time he felt pleasant things filling him and his feet fairly flying along the city streets, which he had hitherto wandered in a mood of hopelessness and angst.

The clerk walked very fast, greeting everyone and making rude remarks to strange men with bohemian faces, while looking behind him from time to time to see if Aziz Bey was coming. They were progressing towards the city's nightlife. The clerk stopped in front of a highly decorative, low door with Arabic writing in shiny letters. He pushed the door open and signalled to Aziz Bey. They went down some steep steps and came to a large area divided into sections by columns covered with mirrors. A few feeble lights lit this dark basement decorated in burgundy velvet; the nightclub that had long since sent home the clients of the night before was preparing for its new patrons.

Aziz Bey looked around; there was a lack of feeling inside him. A little later a well-built Arab, moustache and hair sparkling with brilliantine, wearing a pin-striped suit and waistcoat appeared along with a few well-fed men. Pointing here and there, he was giving some orders in a loud voice in words that were a mixture of Arabic and French. He was attentive, he was firm. When he saw the clerk his face softened. They embraced and began to talk immediately in loud voices, laughing heartily from time to time.

Aziz Bey had shrunk terribly, he had crumbled. His shoulders had fallen, his head was spinning slightly. He thought he was melting in the shadow of this huge Arab. He swayed. At that moment he felt the clerk's hand on his shoulder. Both looked at Aziz Bey and began to speak. The clerk's face revealed his respect for, and praise of, Aziz Bey, but at that moment Aziz Bey failed to understand this; he was too alone and estranged from everything to understand and be happy. The Arab took a cigarette from his case and lit it and his signet ring dazzled Aziz Bey for a moment. He addressed Aziz Bey with a pleasant expression on his face. He made rapid movements in the air with his large-fingered hands as if he wanted to explain something.

But Aziz Bey, a cock crowing in his own dunghill, a lion in his own neighbourhood, clever, proud, even conceited, did not understand a word of what the two men were saying. He just looked. Finally the clerk could not stand it, took the tambur and thrust it into Aziz Bey's hands. It was then Aziz Bey understood that they were asking him to play. The clerk pulled up a chair, Aziz Bey sat down and began to play the tambur that had been placed between his knees.

> The heart is tired now of shedding tears with your love.
> Because there are no tears left in the eye, it has sobered with patience now...

He shut his eyes tightly to stop the tears falling. In spite of his hands trembling and his voice sounding tearful, the Arab smiled with pleasure and the clerk was looking at Aziz Bey with a broad, stupidly naïve smile, as if taking pride in this work of art. The song ended, the big burly Arab patted Aziz Bey on the back patronisingly, as if praising a child who had memorised his times tables well. He smiled and left saying a multitude of words to the clerk. The clerk took Aziz Bey by the hand, brought him over to a corner and seated him down, then disappeared under the gloomy lights.

Aziz Bey was alone, helpless and melancholy. He was tearful. His hand, still grasping the tambur tightly, was sweaty. He was such a stranger to everything, he could not find even a tiny clue to help him understand his state. He could not even think of a face-saving interpretation to enable him to sit up straight on the burgundy velvet chair. His face was as sad as a child who had lost his mother in a crowd and was waiting for her to find him. No doubt if he had seen this childish, tearful, deprived expression, that pitiful state would never have been erased from his memory, and his relatively short life would have been even more brief. But luckily there was not enough light for him to see himself in the broken mirrors that covered the columns from top to toe.

A little later, a waiter left a tray on the coffee table in front of him. Two round flat loaves, a few meatballs and a little green salad. Aziz Bey did not even consider it an offering made out of pity for a poor stranger. Yet although he was fainting with hunger, he ate the food unhurriedly, ridding his mind of any thought of pride. A few hours later, the lights of this vulgar place glitz brightened, and the tables began to fill up. Aziz Bey was lost in contemplation of these sweaty, noisy men of this baking hot land, happy in their own world.

While he was watching them swallowing the drink they had poured into small glasses, watching their smiles, their hearty laughter, and their constant embracing of their long haired, tired women with greasy-looking complexions, he heard a sentence right in his ear.

'You are the one from Turkey?'

He started. A slim, handsome young man with a very thin moustache stood smiling in front of him. They were about the same age. While Aziz Bey was searching his mind for an explanation for this scene the young man had already drawn up a chair and sat next to him.

'So a tambur? And one with a bow too.'

An excited delight appeared on Aziz Bey's face. The deepened, hardened lines that had formed, and resembled a dried corpse in the desert, softened and he smiled.

'With a bow...' he said 'Left by my grandfather...'

The eyes of the Armenian filled as he put out his hand and touched the tambur. He looked at Aziz Bey. It was as if he was not looking at a poor foreigner far from his homeland, but at a souvenir of Istanbul. An inappeasable longing appeared on his face.

'What part of Istanbul are you from?' he asked.

'From Samatya. Do you know it?'

'Don't I just? It's near our place. I'm from Kumkapı... My name's Toros.'

With these words that fatal foreignness in Aziz Bey blew away and vanished like cigarette smoke slowly escaping from an open window; he relaxed. It was not as if they were seeing each other for the first time, but were two childhood friends that had grown up in the same street.

The sweat-bathed musicians had taken a break from entertaining the merrily sizzled patrons in that complicated language with its strange intonation and unaccustomed melody. Now, there was a loud hum all around. While the Arab boss wandered among the customers with an attentive look, the waiters carried mezes and drinks on large trays to the tables, from which bursts of laughter, belches, misty guttural words, startling shouts mingled together, and a careless vibrancy carried on heedlessly. Aziz Bey and Toros – who'd fled from Turkey for a crime he had committed six years earlier – stared at and talked to each other non-stop, in a mood in complete contrast to the others. At that moment, homesickness had bound them together, as though making them blood brothers. They had a feeling of humiliated partnership brought about by having walked the same streets, boarded the same trains, cat-called at the same girls, and sworn with the same words.

'Are they still eating blue fish?' asked Toros. 'It's been six years since I've tasted an Istanbul blue fish.'

That night, Aziz Bey started to play in the tavern of Toros from Istanbul, where Armenians who had emigrated from Turkey regularly went, occasionally bringing with them large bosomed, long-legged, pale-skinned Arab Christian girls in low-cut dresses, young enough to be called children. It was poorer and less showy than the Arab's tavern. But it was tremendously exciting. The patrons attacked Aziz Bey's music like a glass of water.

Even if the music in the tavern awoke in Aziz Bey's soul a state to be pitied, a feeling of being an orphaned child; singing songs about Istanbul reinforced the longing he felt for the city and increased his desire to stay alive and return to his country. There came a moment when he forgot that there were thousands of kilometres between him and his beloved city and when he went outside he thought that he would find himself in the rough cobbled streets of Samatya, where a strong sea wind blowing would carry the smell of seaweed to his nostrils and if he listened carefully to the silence of the city he would hear small ripples beating very softly against the shore.

*

38

Many years later, after Aziz Bey had really become Aziz Bey, one night when he was alone, he had sat down and made an account of his life, and written about the first night he played in Toros' tavern in both columns. Toros was the only person in Aziz Bey's life to whom he felt both great gratitude and whom he would have preferred never to have met. It was Toros who had appeared suddenly in front of him just at a moment when all his hopes were exhausted, had prevented Aziz Bey from falling from the threshold of misery into the darkness of non-existence.

Yet it was the offer made that night by the same Toros that marked the route he was to take for the rest of his life. It was still the same Toros who was the instigator of his taking the step into this unappreciative, ungrateful, disloyal profession, entertaining drunks whose souls changed like their faces as the bottles emptied. Drunks who did not know how to behave, but went on crying, shouting, vomiting, laughing or becoming aggressive. This way, he became content with whatever tips this noisy, worthless gang felt like giving, turning music into a plaything in the hands of drunks, making it louder from time to time to increase the euphoric atmosphere and like a beggar expect something in return for this strange entertainment.

This feeling of inferiority created by this job had so hardened Aziz Bey that for the rest of his life, even in the most important moments when he should have been compliant, modest, or humble, he had always failed. If asked, he'd deny that this superior, obstinate manner ever hurt him.

Until that tragic incident that took place in Zeki's tavern.

Every night for roughly six months, at a quarter to ten, he got onto a fairly high stage, sat on a wooden chair, placed his tambur between his knees and opened the night with a taqsim overture. At daybreak, he got up from his wooden chair and on his way back to the hotel he counted backwards the number of days still to go; not 99, 98, 97..., but 1, 2, 5, 56, 73, 144... He was counting an unknown number of days. He knew both the east and the west of this city that was yet to be divided either in people's minds or on the map. He saw too that this city's weather could become cooler, and that its cats ate from rummaging in the rubbish bins. He got used to its cooking. While looking out of the window of the disintegrating hotel, absorbed with the washing hanging from the balconies of the multi-storied apartments, he kept thinking of his own streets.

A few days a week he went to the port. He looked for a ship where he could again pay his passage, where there were people who understood his language; but he could not find one. Almost every time he went down to the port he learnt that a Turkish ship had weighed anchor either a few hours or a few days before. He began to believe that his destiny would end in this hot city where he sensed the smell of the desert behind the mountains on his skin. As he took each sip of arak he missed the full-bodied rakı that satisfied his palate. He wrote a few letters to his mother and father, but never received a reply. He was tired of playing and singing the same songs. He deciphered many words of that complicated language mingled with Arabic, French, Armenian and Turkish. During his first days of work, when, as he played the taqsim overture, a few enraptured music – lovers would generously and ostentatiously leave bank notes in a copper pot that stood immediately in front of the stage, he felt the blood that was flowing through his veins rush to his head, and his face flush. Later he got used to this feeling. He gradually hardened as if frozen.

It was already the third or fourth week since he had begun working. He lost track of time in this tavern where gigantic fans hung from the ceiling and where electric fans dotted here and there turned without ceasing; where trays were delivered seventy types of mezes on tables set with an eye for showiness. He would not keep track of time because he kept mixing up the days, and he forgot the number that he had counted of days to go; every night he started counting again. Towards evening, he got up from the sleep that had knocked him out at dawn. He washed his hands and face and sat for a while on his bed. There was still a lot of time before going to work. He was in the convalescent period of his love sickness, trying to forget his hurt, his great mistake. This hell city that he had fallen right in the middle of by, his own fault, had embraced him in spite of this. He felt a strange gratitude towards the city; he felt that if he left one day he would leave a piece of his heart here. He wanted to go out of the hotel whose clerk he had become close friends with, with whom he even played backgammon from time to time, pass through the streets whose ins and outs he had learnt, and walk along the magnificent wide roads lined with giant palms and luxury hotels.

His clothes were falling apart and he had lost weight. The old Aziz Bey, wouldn't have dreamt of leaving the house if he couldn't find a tie to match his shirt; he'd toss aside his trousers if they hadn't been ironed with a double crease, and his handkerchief starched. It would never have occurred to the old Aziz Bey that he one day he would wander upmarket roads in wrinkled trousers and a faded shirt, tieless, handkerchief-less, with drooping shoulders and dull eyes, like poor children watching garden cinemas from the top of the wall...

In actual fact, he did notice how shabby he'd become, not that he cared. He had accepted this sorry state as being a necessity of foreignness. Knowing that all he suffered was part of the act of survival made him feel better, and he hoped one day he would return to his own city and be delivered from this sorry state. He walked very slowly in the shadow of the high, smart buildings, his eyes searching the sea as if looking for a ship that would take him away. The costly beauties of the city dazzled his eyes.

An expensive convertible drove past him, and stopped in front of one of the luxury hotels. A young man dressed in spotless white and a young girl with curly black hair got out. Aziz Bey thought for a moment his heart would stop beating. He went weak at the knees and leant against the wall. He looked carefully at the girl as the couple walked into the hotel with easy, carefree steps. Then he shut his eyes.

'Thank God...'

Despite having the same hair, the same air, the same style even, the girl was not Maryam. He sank to the ground and stayed for a while with his head in his hands. He was shaken by the possibility of seeing Maryam in such a smart car with such a pompous, confident, handsome young man; Maryam who, after drawing him to her like a poisonous spider, had reneged on all the promises made in fancy sentences in letters of pink paper, ridiculed all his hopes relating to the future. This scene that ran before his eyes engraved in his mind the bitter truth that Maryam had left him quietly and carelessly. This time he understood for certain that for Maryam all this had been a sweet daydream that never needed to come true. He decided to erase from his mind that unfaithful sweetheart with the black hair that flew hither and thither in the wind.

But it wasn't to be. Despite dedicating all the years of the rest of his life to forgetting Maryam, and striving to overcome the distress in his soul caused by her indifference and disloyalty, he failed. His heart ached like a wounded place that would not heal, letting a thin trickle of blood flow from time to time. This wound sometimes became an ache, sinking inwards, and sometimes became an anger that overflowed. He never saw Maryam again, he never once came across a trace of her; he never heard a word about her. Yet he couldn't forget her. Maryam always existed next to him like a doppelgänger. She was like revenge yet to be taken, a lover with whom to be reunited, a never-ending longing; she was an overflowing mixture of all feelings at once. But Maryam had no inkling about any of this.

True, he never managed to save enough money for the train, or find a ship to take him back home, as soon as possible, because in the end his heart wasn't truly in it.

If he had really wanted to, he could have slipped a couple of piasters into the hand of the walrus-moustachioed official sitting in the shade at the port smoking a shisha, once he'd learnt a little of that language shouted on the streets, and boarded a ship. He could have looked out on his dear city's faded but beautiful silhouette when he looked from the deck on a warm autumn day. There was a reason for his looking at the employee smoking a shisha and moving away, for his somehow not wanting to go. He had hidden this reason in the most secluded corner of his heart and mind; he even denied it at times when he was on his own.

He waited with the hope of meeting Maryam suddenly one day on an unlikely street corner and asking, 'Why did you deceive me? Why did you beg me to come and then leave me high and dry?' Without giving her the opportunity to answer he would say 'Wipe *me* from your memory too.' Yes, he lived for six months with this hope, his eyes scanning the terraces of luxury hotels, his pulse racing whenever he saw a young lady pass by with curly black hair flying about in the wind.

Those six months were difficult to live through. Whenever he saw a policeman in the distance he changed his path, he entertained rich and capricious drunks who wished to quench their longing for their native land with music. He took his share of the tips in the copper bowl that was emptied out onto the table after everyone had left, while the lights were being turned off one by one. His hands always trembled as he took it. He was never quite satisfied, never slept soundly.

But finally he realised that Maryam did not pass along the streets he walked all day long, that the few harsh words at the tip of his tongue had almost gone mouldy, and that the streets of Istanbul passed one by one before his eyes in the dirty bed into which he climbed as the day dawned. It was then that he decided to return.

Winter had come. From time to time a dirty, fine, soaking rain smothered the city's streets in mud. One night, Aziz Bey returned to his hotel after the programme, washed his hands and face and sat on his bed. He looked outside and thought for a while in this unheated, wretched hotel room. He got cold, he pulled the second-hand coat that he had bought from a street seller across his shoulders and counted the money that he had pinned to his vest. There was a strange emptiness inside him. This money would be enough for him to buy a ticket if he travelled on deck. His first job the next morning was to go and purchase that ticket.

The following night, the programme ended, the drunks dispersed in ones and twos, and the place was tidied up. Aziz Bey sat down beside Toros, who was drinking with a sad expression at the table under the only light left on in the tavern. He filled a glass with arak.

'Toros,' he said 'I'm going back to Istanbul now. I've bought a ticket, for a boat...I'm going.'

A deep silence had fallen on the place; it was as though it were completely deserted.

Toros looked at Aziz Bey with eyes instantly filling with tears.

'To Istanbul eh?' he said. 'When?'

'In about a week.'

They did not speak for a while. Aziz Bey swallowed.

'Thanks Toros,' he said 'If it hadn't been for you, I would have died in this foreign land.'

Toros smiled.

'Don't be silly,' he said.

A waiter brought peeled bananas and oranges to Toros' table. Toros filled the glasses. He sighed with a groan.

'Istanbul,' he said, 'Istanbul. Will I see her again? Who knows?'

Aziz Bey took his tambur and began to play. Toros started to sing with a low voice that only the two of them could hear.

> You are my flower of passion, my precious crown.
> You've no idea how much I love you...

That night they did not sleep.

On the morning of the day of the journey, Aziz Bey woke up early. Through the dirty windows of his room he looked at the city made to glisten in places by a refracted sunlight. He was sad.

He knew that he would never see this city again, this place where he had learnt the bitterest lesson of his life. He recorded every little detail in his memory, he put his tambur and everything he had acquired in that city – a new shirt, a second-hand coat, a few pairs of socks, shaving set, a few singles – into a suitcase and left the hotel. He breathed in the air that had become cool but was still smelt of spices and flowers.

Arriving at the port with Toros, they embraced under the big shadow of the ship.

'You're going to eat blue fish in Balıkpazarı, don't forget!' said Toros. 'Grilled, though, all right?'

'Alright,' said Aziz Bey. 'And for desert it I'll eat halva for you. From Koska. With pistachio nuts.'

As he climbed the ladder let down from the ship, Toros was wiping his eyes with the back of his hand, 'Say hello to Istanbul!' he yelled, 'Greet Istanbul for me!'

Aziz Bey leant on the rail and waved to Toros for a long time. After the deep muffled sound of a horn, the ship weighed anchor, and the tall, muscular, handsome figure of Toros slowly became smaller, until it was just a speck. Aziz Bey thought the only good thing that he retained after this strange adventure was to have left a friend in that city who wiped his eyes after bidding him farewell. He was gutted, as if carrying a heavy stone inside himself through the entire journey.

An icy hard February snow had covered the port of Istanbul. As he walked, it crushed with a crunch under his feet. Aziz Bey stopped and bent down to the ground, took a handful of crystallised snow from the bottom of a wall and rubbed it on his face. To feel its coldness on his palms, on his skin, made his burning head feel better. He was crying. He just stood there with tearful eyes as the others disembarked from the ship: passengers reunited with their loved ones, bags and cases passed him by and went. Now there was a new life in front of him. A life unknown, pregnant with days as good as those at the beginning of the adventure or as bad as those at the end. Yet being a native of that life, he was not deterred. He just had to decide where to go.

This void that he fallen into, this feeling of homelessness was upsetting, strange, a little bad; but not at all without hope. It was as though he knew all the people passing by around him. This cold weather, the frost, the wind that lashed like a whip; these sounds, the whistles of the steamers, the hums, the clouds; he recognised every aspect of the city. He was now among people who, if he said 'I'm dying,' would understand what he was saying. The heavy weight of foreignness lifted from him, he began to walk towards the first place he could, his father's house. He walked very slowly; because he had missed his own language, he read all the signs that caught his eye with relish and inhaled the city that he had longed for so intensely. Seagulls were wheeling in the air, buses and trams passed; children selling newspapers were yelling; women with umbrellas and men with raincoats were trying to get to places in time. To him the city seemed like a loving mother prepared to take him to her bosom.

He arrived shamefaced in front of the door that, on leaving the house, he had slammed, bringing down the frosted glass. He was ashamed of everything. He was very ashamed of having imagined he was loved and having been mistaken. He would have preferred to die if he could. Life had taught him a far greater lesson than his father had wished, had taught him a far graver lesson than he had deserved.

Well, had Aziz Bey learnt his lesson?

No... Aziz Bey, like many others, had preferred to grapple with, and defy life.

His forefinger remained indecisive for a while on the bell. A strong wind was blowing; it sliced his face and the back of his neck. His body that for six months had grown accustomed to a hot climate shivered violently, partly because it did not know what it should expect. Aziz Bey overcame his indecision, even though he knew he would be rebuked, and timidly pressed the bell like an acquiescent child. He listened to the footsteps coming from inside. These weary, tired, shuffling sounds were nothing like his mother's hurried steps.

His father opened the door. They stared at each other for a few seconds. When Aziz Bey saw the state of his father he was dumbfounded. Before him stood an exhausted man, whose lined face showed the anticipation of death. He was skeletal. His eyes had sunken in, and his dishevelled hair and beard had become snowy white. He looked unkempt. The striped pyjamas that he was used to seeing him in only at night were filthy; a yellowing vest peeked between the half done up buttons. Aziz Bey gaped at this sorry and decrepit scene and was just about to say 'Father...' when hatred flashed in the still lively eyes of this corpse-like body, and his father shut the iron door in Aziz Bey's face. He could not get his father to open that door again.

He learnt what had happened during his absence the first night that he stayed in the house of his aunt who, despite her deep fondness for him, still looked angry. He stirred and stirred a steaming bowl of paprika soup. He had no appetite. He was so afraid of what he was going to hear that he had forgotten his hunger and his tiredness, his long journey spent on the deck on a bare board, and all his pain. He just did not have the courage to ask about his mother. They were silent. The sound of the kettle boiling on the stove commanded the entire room.

Suddenly, his aunt blurted out, 'Your mother died. The day you left...'

The water boiling over from the kettle dripped and sputtered on the stove. Aziz Bey felt like ice in the room where the coal stove burned red hot. He said nothing, and left the table without touching his food.

'I feel very sleepy,' he said 'I'm tired...'

That her nephew had not had a bite to eat did not escape his aunt's notice; she made up a bed on the couch in the room where the stove was burning. Aziz Bey lay on the bed and buried his face in the pillow. He slept immediately. When his aunt entered the room the next day, she found Aziz Bey unconscious. He had a high fever. His breath was moist to the point of being steamy. He lay for about a month in his aunt's house.

Aziz Bey had always been an obstinate man, what he said went; he had never been seen to bow and scrape, beg or plead. Despite all the harshness of his character, however, he tried very hard to make peace with his father. He went to his house time after time. He rang the bell for ages; he waited with patience for the door that was shut in his face to open. Each time the net curtain of the window that looked out onto the street was parted slightly, but the door whose glass Aziz Bey had broken as he left did not open.

And so the Aziz Bey who was the cause of the incident that occurred in Zeki's tavern was the same Aziz Bey in whose inner being such a touching story had opened a wound that would not heal. He spent a lifetime trying to suppress the pain of that wound, to exaggerate the headstrong, even arrogant attitude in his nature, to insolently oppose the heavy blow that life had dealt at such a young age.

In the end no one emerged on top in this tragic story.

After his return, his life changed completely. He was never again the cheerful, irresponsible youth who revelled in love. He did not even get in touch with his old friends. Nor did he often walk around the streets where he had grown up. Didn't whistle in the streets. Wasn't filled with the joy of life as the day dawned.

Just played the tambur until he got cramp in his wrist. Started and lost a lot of jobs. He could not stay long in the house of his aunt, who blamed him for his mother's death. He rented a room in a boarding house in Aynalıçeşme. When he awoke each morning in that room, whose heavy damp smell permeated all his belongings and which looked out onto a dark narrow street, he thought how alone he was and went out into the street in this melancholy frame of mind.

He was young, fairly good looking and knew how to behave and talk. Because of this he had access to many places and many jobs, but he immediately got fed up with the boorish managers and their easy-going assistants in those low-ceilinged offices; he made no attempt to learn the job they gave him, felt an overwhelming desire to go out at once into the fresh air or to return to the city's quiet streets. He could not get used to being told off, or to taking orders. When they sent him out on an errand, he'd return in four hours instead of half an hour and make it very obvious in every way that he was waiting eagerly for work to finish. So he never lasted long in any job. He was even more headstrong and conceited than before.

At one point, because offices, shops, depots and stores depressed and bored him, he tried his hand at manual labour. He thought that if he exhausted himself with physical work all day, he would be able to forget this strange sorrow that had enveloped his soul. He began to work on a building site. But that didn't last very long either. The foreman tried to slap him for toppling a wheelbarrow full of bricks and in return Aziz Bey gave him a thorough working over, and quit.

He began to frequent a tavern in Tarlabaşı. If he had the money he paid the bill, if not he had it put on tab. It was a quiet place with one or two innocuous, poor, melancholy patrons. He used to go there almost every evening and occasionally take his tambur with him. The evening of the day he beat up the foreman, he was broody. Seeing him in this state, the tavern keeper came and sat beside him.

'Son,' he said, 'what do you keep thinking about? You've got a valuable skill there. My place is too small, but we can find a place that would want you.'

That night Aziz Bey thought hard. There was good reason while he was far from home, when there was no other way to stay alive. While he was there he either had to play or die. But in his own city, in the taverns where he regarded himself a local, where he felt as if he were the landlord, to entertain drunken patrons who didn't know how to behave, to touch the strings of this valuable musical instrument to suit their contemptible desires...

But he realised he had no alternative. The only thing he knew how to do properly in this life was to play the tambur. And so he began playing in taverns.

After making this very difficult decision, his luck changed for the better. Aziz Bey had been to many places before he came to Zeki's tavern; he passed through bars, nightclubs and music halls. He even became known as *Tamburî* Aziz Bey; so respected was he by virtuosos and patrons alike. And so it was that during those years he felt a lot better. He frequently came to forget the blow he had received from Maryam.

At a time when he still lived in the worst room of the pension and while he made do with food stuffed down during the programme intervals instead of a proper meal, a job offer came from a somewhat better tavern. The offer was not bad. For a start he would not have to play until the early hours of the morning, and apart from the tips collected by the drummer and clarinettist, he would have a small wage of his own. He accepted almost immediately. A hope, if only small, that everything was going to get better, kindled inside him.

Although he never thought his father would see him again, he still went on visiting the man whose heart had turned to stone with resentment for his son. Each time the same thing happened. A few days a week he used to go to his father's house at different times hoping to catch him unawares and ring the bell for ages. After parting the curtain and looking for a few seconds, his father would disappear again. Aziz Bey knew that this stubborn, disgruntled man was staring at him from behind the curtain. And so he'd sit in front of the pane for about half an hour, fix his eyes on the window and wait without moving; sometimes he wrote little notes on paper and stuffed them under the door.

At times like these, his inside became as dry as a desert. He didn't feel guilty for having left home all that time ago, but the pain of not having been able to explain it.

That day he went to his father's house with fresh hope. He rang the bell and then waited for that movement that he was used to seeing at the window. He was waiting for the net curtains, now gone grey because they had not been washed since his mother's death, to part, and to see his father's eyes for a moment and the curtain would close again.

But although he waited for quite a while, the curtain was not parted. Aziz Bey felt as though a vein had burst in his breast and filled with blood. He smashed the window with a huge stone he picked up from the ground, then climbed inside through the window in front of which his mother had in the past arranged flowers in pots and out of which, leaning on a cushion, she anxiously watched her son playing in the street, and which had closed on the happy days as he grew up.

His father was sitting stiff as a board in his chair, wearing the same pyjamas as always and his reading glasses, and holding a newspaper. On the table was a frying pan with some half-eaten garlic sausage and egg, and the dried end of a loaf of bread. A few garments that had been washed were hanging on a line strung across the room. He heard a song rising in murmurs from the radio that had been left on for who knew how many days.

There is no wound as painful as the wound dealt by words.
There is not a cure in the world for the wound of the heart

A hot, dry pain flared inside. His tear ducts were burning red hot, like a riverbed dried under the sun. He was filled with a desire to stretch out his trembling hands to close the eyelids of this elderly corpse. Now there was no trace of the resentment in the eyes that until recently had looked like fire. It was as though a dulled pair of dirty marbles lay in the eye sockets of a stranger. When he touched his father's hardened eyelids, with the reality of death he felt he had been left entirely alone on the face of the earth. He was now alone like a seed that had not fallen to its bed of earth but had stuck and dried between two pieces of stone. All this passed through his mind; yet he realised he had been waiting for such independence, and even desired it. In fact, he had never really minded his father's lasting reproach for in all truth, it was he who never forgave his father.

When he deserted this house he'd seen numb, defeated, spent expression in his mother's eyes as she looked at his father, and had realised she'd been hurt irreparably. That it was not him, but his father whom his mother had not forgiven comforted him. This old man who'd spent his life blustering and thundering about must have seen that hurt face, but had chosen to foster a deep resentment instead of wasting away accepting he'd founded an entire lifetime on mistaken principles. That was the reason this picture of death before his eyes hurt Aziz Bey twice over. The house now reeked of a strong smell of damp mixed with misery left over from so many vanished emotions.

He took his father's suit that, so well preserved thanks to his mother's ministrations, a pair of shoes, reading glasses and a felt hat, and gave away the rest of his father's belongings to the neighbours.

The next evening he donned his father's smoke grey suit, starched shirt and tie, and began his programme with a little bit of his father inside him.

> Will this wound in my heart not find a cure?
> Now all is pitch black in my suffering heart.

As he wore that suit, he somehow became reconciled with his father, and shared in his guilt.

*

For many years after this death, there were no important changes in his life. Time, and the sound of his tambur soothed everything. He moved up two floors in the boarding house he lived in to a larger, light and airy room; he ate at the right times, he bought new underwear, handkerchiefs and socks. A multitude of women came and went through his life just as they had before Maryam. He made new friends and acquaintances and began to laugh and talk happily, even if not quite as much as in his early youth. He approached middle age as a handsome man; a maturity and a worldliness entered his attitude and manner. Yet he kept aloof, and when job offers came along he did not hurry, but worked meticulously until he gradually became known in his own small field and gained respect. One day they called him from a top-notch nightclub. 'Play at our club,' they said. He thought it over and accepted. That day he saw the notice 'unfinished suit for sale' in the window of the blind tailor. His father's suit was well worn by then, and while he was still thinking, 'Should I get that suit?' he went in and bought it.

It was a striking black lounge suit with a purple satin collar and cuffs. When he returned to his room, he put it on and looked in the mirror. The body was a perfect fit but the sleeves were too short. Neither was it finished yet. The tacking was still in place. He went to Macide Hanım who ran the boarding house.

'Do you know of a good tailor?' he asked. 'I need to have this suit finished. The sleeves need lengthening a little too.'

Macide Hanım examined the costume on Aziz Bey, looking at it from every angle.

'There's not much left to do,' she said. 'Vuslat will finish it in a couple of nights. She's my niece... If you like I'll call her, let her have a look at it. Actually she's a typist in a firm, but she's good at sewing.'

'Is she skilled enough to do it?' he asked. 'She mustn't spoil my beautiful suit...'

'This is nothing Aziz Bey,' said Macide Hanım. 'She even sews her brothers' winter coats, surely she can sew this?

'In that case would you kindly call and let her come?' said Aziz Bey.

Vuslat came that same evening. She was a tiny, pale girl past her prime; she was timid. Aziz Bey appraised her coldly and impudently.

'I don't want any mistakes,' he said. 'Just so you know. Don't even begin if it's beyond you.'

Vuslat was confused, not knowing how to respond. Just then, Aziz Bey noticed her eyes; those of a girl past her prime, who stood as if wallowing in deepest grief. They sparkled, those eyes put in with a smutty finger. Aziz Bey saw these eyes about to fill with tears, and regretted his harsh manner.

'Iron it well,' he said, 'I'm very particular.'

That night at the tavern, Vuslat popped into his mind from time to time. Her quietness, calmness, the sense of sadness in her gaze wrenched him deep inside, and he regretted his harsh treatment.

Chatting to his friends that day, they got round to the subject of women, and their infidelity. Again Aziz Bey remembered Maryam, and relived that painful adventure. On Tuesday, when he took the suit from Macide Hanım and was putting it on, he lost his temper for no reason, found a stack of faults, and ranted and raved. He wanted the seamstress – whose name he knew perfectly well was Vuslat – to put them right immediately.

Macide Hanım was astonished; she could see none the faults Aziz Bey complained about.

'I'll tell her and she'll put them right, Aziz Bey,' she said. 'Why lose your rag over this?'

She stared after the departing Aziz Bey complete with his suffocating fury; and didn't understand a thing.

The next evening Aziz Bey – all he'd said about the newly finished suit long forgotten – was wound up with the excitement of the nightclub. He was working on one of his new songs. There was a knock at the door. It was as though a nervous, frail hand, hesitant about whether or not to knock was touching the frame.

Aziz Bey opened the door and saw Vuslat.

'I've brought your suit...' she said.

She was holding the slightly wet packet wrapped in sheet upon sheet of newspaper to her breast inside her coat; she drew it out and presented it to him. There was no one around. There was not a sound from the rooms, the only audible noise being the rain beating violently on the windowpanes. Aziz Bey noticed that water was dripping from her coat hem. He likened the girl to a frightened sparrow struggling in a rough hand.

'Come inside,' he said. 'You're soaked.'

Vuslat was uneasy. After all these years spent quietly and unobtrusively trying to avoid attention, she was both very afraid and longing to enter the strange and troubled field created around this man who seemed larger than life to her, with his self-confident manner, his striking movements and his growing popularity as a musician.

'No thanks,' she said in a barely audible voice. 'I'll wait in my aunt's room. If you could try it on and see if it's alright...'

Aziz Bey smiled warmly at the girl whose heart he'd broken a few days earlier with his harsh manner.

'Your aunt isn't there,' he said. 'She's staying on the other side tonight. Come inside and warm up a bit, you're like a drowned rat, come on.'

That night, when he took a book and lay on his bed, he could not stop thinking about the unattractive, puny, but clear-faced Vuslat. There was something good and calming in her bearing and her face, as well as in her soft voice. When Aziz Bey's destructive glance fell on her eyes it paused, he broke inside, and a feeling of loving compassion towards this forlorn, subdued face kindled inside him. A poor lonely girl forgotten in her own narrow world in this city where everyone suffered his or her own individual trials... And then the thought struck him that he was at least just as lonely as her. He had no home, no family. The years that passed without one realising would pass even quicker; the troubles and sorrows he had hidden to be able to hold his head high and remain proud would gradually become more unbearable. A life woven with friends, food, drinking sessions, propositions, interviews, patrons and a stack of other details enveloping him from all directions as soon as he took a step outside his room, took on a totally different aspect when he entered his room and closed the door; then a childish wistfulness settled on that confident, busy, Aziz Bey and he felt the need for someone who would listen intently to at least a few words of what was bottled up inside.

Could this person possibly be Vuslat? He had no desire and was in no fit state to fall in love, to put up with whims or satisfy the heart of a woman who would turn their mutual lives into a silly rhyme of never-ending demands. Such was his selfish reflection that he thought he could only live with a woman like Vuslat who was quiet, insignificant, invisible unless peered at carefully, whose presence was not felt unless needed. If he spoke she listened, if he asked she answered; in short he thought he could live with a woman who made life as easy as possible, moreover he wanted such a woman.

He began to think frequently about this. He had Vuslat sew two shirts and a jacket although he did not need them. During the fittings, measurements, and comings and goings, he formed an opinion of her. As for Vuslat, she felt so insignificant beside him, she vehemently avoided crossing his path or of disturbing him by being seen. She was frightened of being swept up in an unfounded hope and being hurt, so she made no move to go beyond the distance Aziz Bey had placed between them. It is very possible that she even avoided dreaming, lest she get carried away and believe in those dreams.

It was on a planned walk during lunch break that they ran into each other. This was no coincidence; Aziz Bey was seated in a small café that overlooked the door of the office building where Vuslat worked, waiting for her to come out for lunch. When he saw her at the door wearing a coat she'd made herself, he left the café, followed her for a while and then approached her and said, 'Hello.' An evident joy flashed over Vuslat's face. They chatted a little. Aziz Bey acted as warmly as he was able. He had worn the jacket she'd made, and he invited her to lunch. He had such a commanding manner that Vuslat could not say no; she made herself think that this was a casual invitation and did not look for an intention that would raise her hopes in vain. They went to a pudding shop and ordered chicken pilaf. Aziz Bey was relating something in a powerful voice; Vuslat was listening with a smiling face. The chicken pilaf was finished and they went on to dessert.

Aziz Bey asked, 'Do you work on Saturdays?' as though it were a natural part of the conversation. 'If you're free, let's go to the cinema.'

Vuslat dropped the pudding spoon, and as she tried to reach it she knocked her glass over.

All she could manage was a stuttering, 'All right...'

As they were leaving, she couldn't even manage to put her coat on, or find the door.

They married within a few months. However much Vuslat's father hemmed and hawed and made feeble objections to the loss of a wage coming into the house; however much her good-for-nothing brothers objected merely for the sake of it, saying, 'We won't give a girl to a musician,' for the first time in her life Vuslat put her foot down saying, 'I'm going to get married.' This obstinacy greatly astonished both her father and her aunt.

During the time they rented and furnished a house overlooking the Golden Horn, Aziz Bey did take some pleasure in life. He thought that from then on he would be living a comfortable, easy existence, but he did not consider this new state very important; whereas all this had passed through Vuslat's head.

Everything was as Aziz Bey wanted it. Their wedding ceremony was extremely simple, as he had not wanted to invite many guests. Vuslat's father, aunt, two very close friends... that was all. This excessive simplicity upset Vuslat. All the same, she did not mind too much, since she just could not believe that she was married to Aziz Bey. The first night she kept waking up to look and see whether or not the man lying beside her was indeed him.

However, it didn't take her long to realise that the only loving party in this marriage was herself. She quickly saw they didn't find the same meaning in their life. There was not a trace of the kind of romantic feelings that filled Vuslat in Aziz Bey. She retreated into the shell she'd readily abandoned in that simple ceremony. And thus that great dream came to an end.

These years were Aziz Bey's heyday. The colourful world outside had embraced and surrounded him. He was happy to abandon himself to this exciting and drunken world where melodies and drink flowed like water, where there was no room for quiet souls. It was as though he were swimming in a hot river, passing over waterfalls, falling into still lakes and finding himself afterwards again among the foam. He loved this fast life that took on a different face each evening. He performed at a number of nightclubs every night, went on tours, watched different women pass through his life, he spent money like water and became drunk in melodies. In this way, he forgot Maryam and the time he spent downtrodden, sad and dejected in a faraway and hot city. That charismatic halo he created around himself grew and strengthened; and Aziz Bey lived vainly, to his heart's content.

While he was out, carried away among the constantly raised rakı glasses, the music and peals of laughter, Vuslat sat in front of the window with deep shadows on her face thrown by the lamp burning in the far corner of the room. She looked at a shattered moonlight reflecting in the dirty waters of the Golden Horn, thinking about her life and grieving. Despite Aziz Bey's objections she had a baby, who did not live. After that she faded altogether, and became silent.

And so they spent many years like this, and both grew old. Vuslat was worn out from carrying her broken heart. Aziz Bey's golden years came to an end. The nightclub owners, who at one time sent cars to collect the famous *tamburî* of the time from his house, closed their businesses one by one. Families withdrew to their homes; outmoded singers unable to keep in step with the new system fell from favour, their hearts ached and they became alcoholics.

Aziz Bey began spending most of his time at home. The friends who at one time dragged him by the arm to musical orgies were hard at work in bad nightclubs and cheap music halls trying to earn a crust. With that splendid life behind him, Aziz Bey's once lyrical and musical life was like a long cheerful coloured film, which faded into a dull photograph. He resisted for a while, but eventually he surrendered. He was reduced to second-class taverns instead of the nightclubs where his capriciousness knew no end. He shared the same fate as his friends.

Not a word passed through their lips at the end of their sessions in the early hours of the morning. Wishing each other goodnight, they scattered home in deep distress, tucking their heads down, pulling the collars of their jackets up. No one offered to spread a table in a tavern for them any longer. Even their subjects of discussion during the short intervals in the programme changed. They stopped talking about the girls who had just come on the market, the scandals that rocked the place, the compositions entering the Turkish Radio and Television's repertoire, the articles in the newspapers about famous singers, their reminiscences of philandering. They even stopped pulling their acquaintances to pieces. They were occupied with wood, coal, rent, gas bills and debts to the local shop. An expression of bewilderment which read, 'How did it come to this?' settled on their faces, a broken strain entered their voices. They became too complaisant and they submitted. In the end, all those true musicians who'd been playing since childhood and who'd never have anything said against the music they played, virtually disappeared.

Drunks who slurred their speech after a couple of glasses asked Aziz Bey to play arabesque songs whose titles he'd not even heard of. He put up with this new turn of events, hoping it would quickly pass, and that he'd soon return to that colourful life. Putting up with it made him, if anything, more intolerant, bad tempered, and even more aggressive than before. A long time passed like this, too.

Things got from bad to worse. Aziz Bey had been unemployed for several months. He had worked in almost all the taverns that employed musicians and the fairly respectable nightclubs; had quarrelled with them all and had left. They were living off their capital. Because it went against the grain to go round begging to his old bosses who had had their nightclubs pulled down and had office blocks built in their place and the organisers who at one time ran after him, he sat at home tense and depressed all day, reading the papers and drinking endless cups of coffee. Sometimes, he would go out onto the balcony and shout at the children playing ball in the neighbourhood, while waiting all the time for the telephone to ring with a good offer just for him.

It was around that time that he caught an inkling of Vuslat's hurt feelings. For the first few weeks of his unemployment he had spent almost every day sitting waiting for work in the musicians' café. But he soon left when he realised that this place was only filled with strange-looking men who'd begun their music careers by playing the darbuka to tourists in Kumkapı at the age of five, and where rummy-o boards were overturned every second on tables covered with green broadcloth to the sound of revolting loud guffaws and obscene oaths. Deciding this poisoned the air was not for him, he left his telephone number to a few trusted people and he returned home.

*

With nowhere left to go, his attention focused on his wife. He saw sorrow in Vuslat's eyes, now lost among crow's feet. One day, around midday, he noticed his wife's hair had turned almost entirely white. He was astonished. At that moment his wife appeared both close and as foreign as if he'd never seen her before. Vuslat was preparing the table for lunch, going to and fro between the kitchen and the room. While Aziz Bey was staring at Vuslat as if looking at an old friend who'd reappeared after years of absence, old and exceedingly worn out, she said in her usual frail voice, 'Lunch is ready.' Aziz Bey heard his mother in this frail voice, the soft tone and the tired steps of his wife bringing the meal to the table, and he shuddered.

But that wasn't all. He glanced at the hands clutching the arm of the chair to get up. His own hands... These hands were just like his father's hands. Suddenly he realised that the grumpy-looking man who'd been wandering around the rooms of this house throughout their marriage was not himself but his father; he was horrified.

Unnoticed, he had become his father. His father, who never bared his heart to his wife, who found life outside the home more important than within, who never understood the heartaches at home, or if he had, ignored them; his face perpetually sour, his voice always loud and ready to reprove...

He saw his face in the dresser mirror. The same broad forehead, stern features, then same sharp gaze... He brought his hand to his hair, and the movement of his arm reflected in the mirror was again his father's. The fingers that touched the combed back silvery hair were his too. The man he'd once left, slamming the door in his face, had entered him and lived there silently for years.

He fell into a strange mood. It hurt him to be the continuation of the man whom he could not forgive for trying to prevent him pursuing far off promises and scattering his youthful hopes. And yet, there was also something of a rarity, a feeling of superiority in this identicality, this similarity like two drops of water. For a moment this state seemed to him like a sign of nobility. In this damned world in which he was searching for a humble place for himself in which to be happy, he felt rooted like an aged plane tree; he felt proud. Then he realised how meaningless this was. He was a poor copy of a man whose life had been spent maintaining that his wrongs were right, trying to be a man he was not, and abusing a quiet and inoffensive woman. He was depressed twice over.

He stared with brimming eyes at his wife, who had now prepared the table and was waiting for him to sit down. 'I'm not going to eat' he said, and went to bed. All the time he pretended to be asleep he thought about his wife. He'd lost her in the house, forgotten her in the armchair in front of the window overlooking the Golden Horn. He'd never wondered what she thought about. When he got up towards evening he planned to say pleasant words to Vuslat, to make up for the years of pain, but they just stayed on the tip of his tongue.

He would have put everything right if the telephone call that he'd been awaiting for months had not come the next day, if he'd had a little more time to think about his wife, or indeed, if the life outside he felt a part of hadn't beckoned him back so hurriedly. But Zeki's offer made him forget this frightening revelation almost immediately.

The next evening Vuslat ate alone. Just as before.

Aziz Bey was very happy in Zeki's tavern. He had regained the respect, which, having been used to for years, he wholeheartedly believed was his due. He was delighted with Bahri and Mercan calling him 'maestro' and saying 'after you, Sir, please,' even though they belonged to rabble he'd belittled with the epithet, 'Kumkapı-raised.' His every wish was their command. Zeki showed an exaggerated respect, laid on an elaborate table after the programme and wouldn't let Aziz Bey go before they'd finished a big bottle of rakı together.

Zeki's drunk tongue mumbled 'Abi, if you had any idea how you've honoured me by accepting my offer' flattered the old master no end, the man whom this offer rejuvenated when he was on the brink of falling into the lap of the pain of being forgotten.

'Abi, you'd never believe it,' he said 'Look, Bahri here's my witness. I intended to ring you so many times. But I just didn't dare. In the end Bahri said one day, 'Go on, phone him, what's the worst that could happen? At worst he'd snap at you. Let him. He's our elder, a maestro, isn't he?' I thought about it and realised he was right. Then I picked up the phone and rang you. Just as well I did.' Repeating the same story, and at every telling of the story Aziz Bey felt he could barely contain himself.

He rejoiced as if he wasn't the one who'd painstakingly kept accounts every day, pen in hand, who'd cocked an ear to the most vulgar popular songs just in case an offer came from the wedding halls in the poorer districts, who was left unemployed and languishing in the musicians' café, all the time Zeki was plucking up the courage. His head, forever surrounded by an arrogant halo, stood even more upright. As he bathed in this sea of respect and interest, he never once remembered his wife's heartache, which he'd briefly glimpsed during that troubled time of unemployment.

True, now he returned home more tired. He had no energy left after the programme to enjoy himself singing and drinking. After having a drink with Zeki and his fill of compliments, he'd wend his way home. He'd find his wife seated in front of the window as always, and believe she was waiting for him. But he never realised Vuslat had given up waiting long ago. She no longer expected anything; it was just a habit of years, staring at the houses whose windows spilled light, and envying the happy lives she believed were enjoyed there.

Thus almost a year passed. The reverence and attention he received in Zeki's tavern became run-of-the-mill. Bahri began to slack off, Mercan to do what he felt like doing. Davut no longer brought his rakı at a nod, or took much notice. The table spread after the programme with different mezes at first gave way to a plate of pickles and cheese at the end of Zeki's small table. All the same, each time he got merrily drunk, Zeki still carried on praising Aziz Bey to the skies.

'If this business still stands, it's thanks to you, abi,' he'd say, 'All these patrons you see come to listen to you!'

When he was drunk his words were sincere, he was filled with admiration for Aziz Bey. At times like that, he could cry without embarrassment. And it was unlike Aziz Bey to act with any modesty; even if those who came did not always listen intently to the music, he was utterly convinced it was he who filled the place.

One holy night, when Zeki feared the place would stay empty, a group of eight to ten people arrived. They were very young and very noisy. It was obvious in every way that they had come out of curiosity. Laughing and talking, they quickly drank the rakı and didn't really listen to the heavy, sedate songs that they were unaccustomed to. They weren't familiar with the rakı culture either; they wanted inappropriate foods and upon hearing they weren't offered on the menu, they sulked. Aziz Bey moved from fine, old-fashioned songs that appealed only to refined souls, to newer, lighter numbers. Seeing the group paid no heed to these new songs either, he was annoyed.

Despite his unshakeable obstinacy he'd learnt through the years to change his repertoire to suit the mood of the patrons, and provided good taste was maintained, he'd make sure the patrons who came to drink and be merry would get the sort of music they would enjoy. He took charge of the programme so masterfully that the patrons would give him their full attention. Those who knew them enjoyed the old songs to the full, while others found themselves delighting in Istanbul songs when they came along. But this young group defied every effort to entice them into the right mood.

In any case, most of the youngsters became drunk as lords

before ten o'clock. One girl started to cry, and two lads got into a scrap. Aziz Bey carried on playing, his usual composure intact, while Bahri strove to keep up. Mercan hadn't yet emerged from the kitchen since he'd gone to stuff himself during the first break. As the quarrel among the group grew, all the good cheer drained out of them. They paid the bill and left, still quarrelling.

'Let's go, mates,' said Zeki, 'Tonight we opened in vain.'

Fed up with playing the same things for years in similar places, Bahri and Mercan fled immediately. Aziz Bey took his tambur, said goodnight to those still there and left.

Although winter had arrived, it was quite mild. A warm southerly blew, wrapping itself around Aziz Bey's neck and face, and fluttering his hair. As he walked home he thought about Vuslat. He was filled with a comfortable, pleasant feeling. He felt he was missing his wife and he wanted to be near her for the first time since he had met her; and that felt a little odd. This unfamiliar mood made him think he must be getting old. How quickly that time of harboured pain and disappointment had passed... now he felt that he didn't quite belong to the life outside, he couldn't keep up with it like before. Now he preferred peaceful silence to all that merriment and laughter, and the exuberant tables with loudly sung songs.

He grasped his tambur and decided to go home and play Vuslat's favourite songs. But when he tried to remember Vuslat's favourite song, he realised he could not. It dawned upon him that he'd never played the tambur to her, that until now he'd never thought it necessary. So he chose a song himself:

> The spring of my love, my first thrill.
> My love, my precious, my dearest darling.

He was so sure of finding his wife sitting in her usual chair when he entered that he was astonished to see the place empty. The stove was out, and the room had gone cold. He called out to her but didn't receive an answer. Then he became uneasy. The possibility that Vuslat might have gone made him freeze. He walked quickly round the house. When he went into the bedroom, to his annoyance, he found Vuslat in bed.

Anger flickered inside him. This was the typical Aziz Bey. Yes, he had chosen the time he wanted to love his wife but, you see, his wife had gone to bed. As if the beautiful things that he had happened to think of had been thoughtlessly rebuffed, he got undressed angrily, put on his pyjamas and got into bed beside her. But he started when he touched his wife's arm during the rough movements created by his anger; Vuslat had a very high fever. It was as though her almost non-existent body, soft and weighed down with all the heartache of a wasted life, was burning up. It was as though Vuslat, who was fading like a depleted battery making the radio sound ever fainter, had given up. Aziz Bey put his face near her head. Her breath reminded him of steam, and a barely discernable moan issued from her dried lips.

He sprung out of bed, put on a cardigan and threw a few pieces of wood onto the stove that was about to turn to ash. Then he went to the kitchen.

Just as his aunt had done, he would wet a cloth in water with vinegar and place it on his wife's forehead and wrists. The sharp smell reminded him of the time he fell unconscious in his aunt's house on his return from that yellow-hot city. He had never forgotten that unwanted smell, which from time to time even trickled into his dreams and hurt his nostrils. Now he decided to at least mollify his inconstant conscience, even if he couldn't make up for those unspoken yet heart-warming words that passed through his mind the day he suddenly noticed Vuslat's hair had gone snow white.

He didn't know where to find the vinegar. He didn't know where to find anything. He'd spent his life in this house with everything served on a platter. After opening and closing all the cupboards, he finally found it and brought a towel. In the soft light of the bedside lamp he placed vinegar cloths on Vuslat's forehead until morning.

At dawn Vuslat opened her eyes, her temperature had fallen a little. Aziz Bey was filled with joy.

'You have been ill, Vuslat,' he managed to say, 'You had a very high temperature, but it's dropped now, don't worry.'

It was the first time his voice reflected heartfelt love. Vuslat's eyes filled with tears. An expression of peace appeared on her ever clear face. Her breath was still very hot.

'Is it morning?' she asked.

Aziz Bey nodded and smiled. He turned off the bedside light. The barely visible, pale light of a day preparing to break gathered behind the curtain. A sweet and hopeful half-light enveloped the interior. Aziz Bey got into bed and cuddled his wife whose fever had abated a little. They slept together.

When they awoke, the day had long since broken; the house was very bright. Aziz Bey lit the stove. He seated Vuslat on the couch in the sitting room, covered her with a blanket and brought her breakfast on a tray. Vuslat had no appetite, but she ate a few mouthfuls and drank some tea so as to avoid upsetting him. Aziz Bey threw some wood on the stove, opened the window for five minutes and aired the room. Then he went to Balıkpazarı and did some shopping, called in at the chemist and bought some medicine. He learnt the ins and outs of the kitchen, squeezed orange juice for his wife, and cooked soup in chicken broth.

While he was doing all this he felt a warm feeling circulating inside. Sadly he'd developed this taste all too late. That it was his fault they'd never spent such tender days wounded him, and even made his eyes water while he was stirring the soup. As for Vuslat, she was astonished; she was afraid that this sweet dream too would rapidly come to an end.

When Aziz Bey returned to the room after preparing the evening meal, working passionately like an ant in the kitchen, he found Vuslat again lying unconscious with a high fever. He thought his wife must have caught a stubborn 'flu and phoned Zeki to let him know he was not coming. In reply, Zeki said, 'No problem, abi' and asked if there was anything he could do. If it were any other time he would have been annoyed that Aziz Bey wasn't able to come, but they were in Ramadan and business was slow.

This time Vuslat's temperature fell quicker. But a week later a taxi came to the door. Zeki, Bahri, and Mercan helped Aziz Bey wrap Vuslat in a blanket and carry out to the waiting taxi. She was admitted to hospital.

Aziz Bey had been used to acting as capriciously as the soloists in the wings, making life hell for the room service in the hotels and earning a considerable amount of money, which he'd spent in pursuit of pleasure, Now he was rushing with test tubes full of blood along the dark corridors whose walls were damp, running across wet floors in the basements of the hospital, waiting in queues in front of doctors' doors. The same Vuslat whom he had never enquired about all these years, he now fed milk with a teaspoon, dunking a biscuit in her tea to try to feed her. He was now wiping her face and hands with a cloth and holding her arm to take her to the toilet. Suddenly, he was very afraid of losing this being whose value he'd come to appreciate too late. The same song kept going through his mind. *I found her late, I lost her soon, life has grieved me deeply...*

In truth, he was just as much afraid of being left all alone as he was of losing Vuslat. When he went home to prepare her food or to get a clean nightdress, he started at every little creak; without her he found a wretched emptiness in the rooms of the house.

The care, attention and compassion Aziz Bey showed in the last few weeks of a tired life weren't enough to save Vuslat. On the third day of Bayram, Vuslat died. She had shown not the slightest effort to get better. Her face seemed to say 'Let this state of melancholy, this unhappiness that has lasted for years end as soon as possible.' She was peaceful because she had entered a road of no return. Aziz Bey had an inkling of this, and it made him feel terrible. At each moment as Vuslat's breath became shorter and she neared death, the same question crossed his mind:

'Did she regret loving me?'

Then he remembered Maryam, and how he never regretted

having loved her despite that fact that she had altered the course of his life with that invitation and no matter how much she'd made him suffer indescribable pain, and he realised that Vuslat had not regretted this one-sided, bitter love either.

The mosque courtyard wasn't terribly crowded. Aziz Bey stood among a few friends, childishly tearful, and realised those splendid days were gone for good and that a definite and merciless loneliness awaited him. Those cheerful sounds that at one time filled his table came to his ear from far away, then dispersed in the cloud-laden air. He had lost everyone and everything. He felt that among these losses the most painful was Vuslat. There was nothing to fill this void. He'd always viewed Vuslat as a shadow, a soft light, a part of the furniture fading in the walls; an object so ordinary that if it went missing its absence would not be noticed... He had not found time to love, or rather, he had never looked for it.

After the burial, Zeki and Bahri came back to the house. They came in and sat for a while. Aziz Bey was confused. He stared at the kitchen door as though his wife would come through at any moment, but he couldn't see the reflection of his wife's calm face in the white tiles, or the shining surfaces of the pots all washed cleaned and lined up. After sitting for a while Zeki got up.

'Abi, don't come to the shop until you feel fit,' he said. 'If you like, go away and have a rest. Don't worry about the money.'

He stared at Aziz Bey's face with sympathy, then hugged him tight. He was really felt pity for Aziz Bey's sorry state. He wondered how this high-spirited man who was suddenly shattered would be able to cope with a solitary life.

Well, it was on that evening that the most crucial part of the story that ended with the tragic incident in Zeki's tavern began.

*

69

On the evening of the funeral, Zeki had hurried to find a violinist to add to the team. The place was heaving, mostly with small groups of men and women over middle age and well immersed in tavern culture. They'd already begun drinking. Davut was wandering among the tables swearing, Zeki was bending over backwards to see to every wish of this crowd, who'd denied themselves throughout Ramadan and were now longing to enjoy themselves. If he saw someone not working properly he shot glances ready to kill; he had put aside being the boss and was helping with the service.

Bahri and Mercan and the new violinist taken their places and the music had just started when Aziz Bey arrived. For a moment Zeki had a strange, unpleasant feeling. Then he berated himself and he tried to be sympathetic; thinking of how Aziz Bey could probably not bare to stay all alone at home. He greeted and embraced Aziz Bey courteously and with great respect. He seated him at his small table. After asking how he was and humouring him, he suggested, 'Abi, perhaps it's best if you don't play tonight; Davut will lay us a table at once, and we'll sit and drink. You'll feel better...'

'I've come to play,' said Aziz Bey, 'There are a lot of songs I've not been able to sing earlier...'

Zeki glanced quickly at the patrons who were champing at the bit to let rip, and then back at Aziz Bey; he was afraid that the melancholy gathering in the abstracted eyes of this old maestro would spread to the patrons. Then, sensing this would be the end of the man if he tried to prevent it, he murmured 'So what! Come what may.'

Aziz Bey joined the saz players with a dignified manner. The violinist who'd rushed over with the hope that perhaps these new bosses would like him and offer a permanent job, may have been put out, but he still he got up respectfully and gave his place.

Aziz Bey sat down, his movements slow and deliberate. He squeezed the tambur between his knees and after a long, melancholy introduction he began his song.

Let me cover and wrap my love in the mourning of the night.
Now you are gone, where can I find and plead with you.
Now I am just like an incurably bleeding wound.
Now you are gone, where can I find and plead with you.

At first the patrons did not want to pay attention to such a melancholy song. However much they liked traditional and poignant melodies, this evening they had come to enjoy themselves. One could read on their faces the wish to be accompanied by lively tunes. Glasses were being filled and emptied. Davut and the busboys carried on rushing around. But soon the sadness in Aziz Bey's voice completely enveloped the atmosphere of this tiny tavern. Not even an hour passed before the patrons filling uncomfortable tables fell into the grip of a sadness that they would never forget. They became lost in thought, disappeared on journeys to who knows which moving memories and abandoned themselves to the melancholy songs.

Aziz Bey sang his songs until he ran out of breath, put down his tambur and wiped his brow with his handkerchief. A wild burst of applause broke from the patrons who had, perhaps for the first time in their lives, come across a melancholy atmosphere that gave so much pleasure. Hearing the applause, Aziz Bey freed himself from the world he'd lost himself in; he stared briefly at the moist eyes fixed on him as if trying to understand what was happening. He remembered the golden years, smiled and bowed his head slightly to the crowd that had been so powerfully affected by the music. Women were quietly wiping their eyes with paper napkins, men were filling their emptied glasses and lighting up cigarettes. Zeki took advantage of Aziz Bey's pause, went round the tables and explained the reason the tamburî sang such emotional songs was that he'd buried his wife today. This explanation increased the patrons' strange pleasure twofold. When the evening ended and they were leaving the tavern, they praised Aziz Bey and offered their condolences. Some thought of the moment when they would experience a similar sorrow, and of what they would do on the night they lost their own partners. Zeki embraced Aziz Bey affectionately. It had been an amazing night of spontaneity. When Bahri was walking with Aziz Bey he struggled to find words to express his admiration while at the same time he felt great pity for this tired man who'd now go home to a cold bed and feel only emptiness beside him.

That night Aziz Bey did not lie in his bed. He curled up on the sofa in the sitting room, and fell asleep crying.

But this melancholy began to lose its charm on the nights that followed.

Aziz Bey imagined himself a ball of fire that ignited everything it touched; he expected this melancholy state to always be reciprocated. But that wasn't to be. This ordinary tavern's patrons that varied from night to night began to get fed up with Aziz Bey's ponderous and gloomy songs. They put up with these sad offerings for a couple of hours, but then they wanted to hear cheerful things that would help shake off the stresses of daily life.

Aziz Bey took no notice of these requests; he wanted to view all the patrons as voluntary witnesses to his sorrow, and not as people who paid for their entertainment. To request cheerful songs was akin to treating him with disrespect. He painstakingly prevented Bahri and Mercan from switching to livelier melodies. He was tied with an unswerving loyalty to the sorrowful journey that drove through his soul. He wandered around the same sorrowful notes; with a great show he threw down the pieces of paper and napkins Davut brought to him, bearing requests for cheerful songs, and even trod on some of them. And when some of the patrons asked for the requests they wanted to hear in a loud voice his anger grew. When they saw their requests had still not been performed by the middle of the night, the customers either got up grumbling or stopped listening to the music and settled down to a happy conversation among themselves full of laughter not at all suitable to Aziz Bey's state of grief.

It was because of this that the place began to fill less and less each night. Those who came were discomfited by Aziz Bey's face, whose sorrow was beginning to be replaced by anger. The complaints increased, annoying Zeki more and more.

One late afternoon, Aziz Bey emptied a box of photographs onto the couch where he was sitting at home. He was looking for his wife's pictures. On the small coffee table beside him there was a glass of rakı, and a few slices of orange. Among the photographs showing him at the seaside, on wide roads, in convertibles, in exclusive restaurants, among famous singers, playing, drinking, laughing, enjoying himself, there was nothing of Vuslat, apart from a few faded photographs taken at their wedding. And from those few photographs, Vuslat stared at him with hurt eyes.

Aziz Bey was on the verge of crying when someone knocked on the door that had not been knocked on for days.

It was Zeki. He intended to warn Aziz Bey that things could not carry on like this, and to tell him he had to play according to the customer's wishes. He'd had enough of Aziz Bey's mournful repertoire, and there was nothing for it but to go and have a word. He did not want to talk to him in the tavern, because he had no desire to upset Aziz Bey, who in any case arrived drunk and whose reaction in front of other people could be unpredictable.

But Zeki never got round to saying anything: Aziz Bey was so delighted at Zeki's arrival that he danced attendance on him; he made him coffee, poured him rakı, seated him down comfortably placing cushions behind him, and told him sincerely how happy he was to see him. Zeki found himself unable to voice what was in his mind to this wretched man who sat drinking rakı in his pyjamas, even though evening was about to fall in this house whose kitchen exuded a smell of cabbage stew. They chatted about this and that, and then he got up and left.

The next day he took advantage of Aziz Bey coming to work half an hour early. He seated Aziz Bey down facing him, to talk in the inoffensive but firm and decisive sentences all that he'd thought about during the day.

'Abi, I have the greatest respect for you,' he began, 'But

don't do this. Look, the patrons have stopped coming to the place. We've now got a reputation as the "gloomy tavern." People are saying one should only go to Zeki's tavern if you want a good cry. Abi please. You can't bring back the dead, pull yourself together now...'

Aziz Bey peered sharply at Zeki. He replied patronisingly in a determined voice:

'I won't debase this music for no-good drunks, Zeki.'

Zeki could not answer. His legs trembled with anger for a while. That night Aziz Bey again insisted on having his own way.

Zeki had no idea what to do, and was simply unable to say 'Abi, don't come in any more as of tomorrow.' Every day he found brand-new phrases of dismissal and arrived at work determined, but while he thought, *I'll tell him during the first interval,* and a little later, *No, after the programme,* the night ended and Aziz Bey left without having been fired. For a while he tried to cold shoulder Aziz Bey, and to pay him late. But none of it made the slightest impression on Aziz Bey.

One day he took Bahri by the arm, and led him outside. They walked for a while.

'Tell him not to come any more,' he said. 'Look: we're all going to go bust together. Speak to him. Let him find somewhere else. That is, if he can.'

'How can I tell him abi?' asked Bahri, 'Fate's already hit him; how can I possibly say to him "That's it, we've stopped doing business with you, don't come any more!" You tell him yourself.'

Zeki angrily let go of Bahri's arm. He hurled a kick at the tin near his foot.

'I can't!' he said, 'If I could I certainly would!'

That evening Zeki decided definitely that after the programme he would cut all relations with Aziz Bey. If necessary he would carry on paying his weekly wage. Just so that he'd stay away and not come in anymore to irritate the patrons with tearful songs.

One or two poor drunks were boozing half asleep, with pickles and melon, a little white cheese and beans in olive oil in front of them. Zeki was ready to cry with anger. He looked at the state of the business and swore. And then the programme –which wasn't all that brilliant anyway – ended. Aziz Bey came to the table as usual and sat down. His face was very pale. He did not look very well. Zeki thought this was just the right time to have a word...

He was just about to say 'Abi, that's enough. You've ruined my precious business...' when Aziz Bey began to cough. It was as though he was choking, he was gasping for breath. Bahri ran and got a glass of water. As Mercan shook him by the shoulders a hoarse wheeze came from Aziz Bey's mouth. He couldn't breathe, and his eyes opened large. Bahri took his arm and led him outside.

'Take a deep breath, abi,' he said, 'Let's go to the hospital if you like...'

Aziz Bey opened his eyes wide and shook his head. Then his fit of coughing abated, it almost stopped. It was cool out. They went inside. Aziz Bey, who sat with difficulty on the edge of the chair, was exhausted. His face was pale but trying to smile, and he whispered,

'I'm fine. Don't worry... It's better.'

Confronted with this scene Zeki again could say nothing, and he looked at Bahri.

'Could you take Aziz Abi home?

Aziz Bey didn't object. He took Bahri's arm and began to walk slowly. He coughed from time to time and doubled up when he did. Zeki leant against the door and stared after them and filled with anguish.

'Now go and tell him, "You're done!"...'

Aziz Bey had caught a chill because he hadn't looked after himself properly. He lay ill at home for quite a while. From time to time Bahri looked in to see how he was, this man who had now really sunk, shrunk even, and in shrinking had reached a state of sad and childish winsomeness. Sometimes he brought Aziz Bey medicine; or he sent his wife to bring him soup cooked and wash his clothes.

Whenever Aziz Bey saw Bahri he cried like a child.

Zeki took advantage of this illness. He had no wish to treat this man ungratefully. He remembered how his music had brought his business to its peak only a year earlier. Although he felt guilty, he knew it couldn't carry on like this. He went to visit Aziz Bey with his arms full. He had taken Aziz Bey's tambur with him to forestall the excuse of getting the instrument to come to the tavern. He knocked and a shrunken, wrinkled faced Aziz Bey opened the door. He was unshaven and looked awful. Yet he was delighted when he saw Zeki, and his face lit up. They walked into the room; Aziz Bey apologised and stretched out on his bed. Zeki sat at his bedside.

'Abi, for us there's nothing more important than your health,' he said, 'You are very precious to us. Don't tire yourself by coming to the shop. I'm like your son. It's my duty to look after you. I'm not going to forget the days that you took my business to its peak.'

The sincerity in Zeki's words made him cry for hours. After he left, he prayed as he took his medicine to get better as soon as possible in order to carry on this loyal boy's work from where he left off.

The night of that tragic incident, Zeki lost his patience.

And yet, it had all been going so well. In the five weeks that Aziz Bey had been ill and resting, Zeki had created a brand new repertoire, added the gipsy violinist to the group, who knew the popular songs so well. He had replaced the curtains and tablecloths, installed an air conditioner and placed advertisements about the brand-new programme in the papers. The results had been immediately visible: a private party, a large group had booked the entire joint that night.

Zeki was greeting his patrons at the door in his best outfit when Aziz Bey arrived carrying his tambour. Zeki couldn't believe his eyes, nor find a single word to say to Aziz Bey's customary face; overconfident and vain as always.

Aziz Bey was wearing his old black costume with purple satin collar and cuffs, and had slicked his hair back. There was colour in his face. Even though he looked good, one couldn't help noticing that he had become thin and very small. Yet in spite of this he'd regained his dignified, upright demeanour. That well-known keenness showed in his gaze.

'How are you Zeki?' he asked patronisingly, 'Have you managed to get along without me then?'

Without waiting for an answer he went inside. Zeki's hands began to shake with anger.

It was not just any man who went inside, it was Aziz Bey. The unchanging Aziz Bey with that strange breeze, that charisma and that proud stance. Again there was a curious halo around him. He asked after Bahri and Mercan in a powerful voice, he asked Davut for some rakı and patted the busboys on the back. He even went into the kitchen and teased the chef.

Zeki stood in the doorway gaping at all that was going on inside. He signalled Bahri, calling him over.

'Where did this old fart spring from?' he asked. The anger in his voice was beyond his control.

'How should I know abi?' asked Bahri, 'He must have got better, just look at him. He's really thin but sharp as anything.'

'Look here,' said Zeki, his voice shaking with rage, 'Take no notice of this pillock, I'm warning you. You play whatever the patrons want. I won't hear of anything else.' He paused and took a deep breath. 'Bahri,' he said, 'I swear, damn it, if anything goes wrong tonight I'll chuck you out, the lot of you. I'm warning you. Look here, I've spent a bloody fortune on this business! I won't have it buggered up!'

Aziz Bey waited patiently at Zeki's table for the programme to start. He took a sip of the rakı that Davut had practically thrown on the table. Zeki sat opposite him. He tried to be calm. At first he even smiled.

'I'm really happy to see you abi,' he said, 'May God preserve you, you look fine. There's colour in your face.'

'I'm fine,' said Aziz Bey, 'I've pulled myself together. I'm of the old stock, son.' Then he glanced around. 'You've polished up the place a lot. It's really nice, well done.'

Again that proud talk, again that arrogant attitude. There was a short silence. Zeki swallowed.

'Abi, I ask you, please,' he said in a half-begging voice. 'This evening the patrons are very special. They made a point of asking that no sorrowful, melancholy songs be sung. Please abi... you won't, will you, otherwise you'll utterly ruin me.'

Aziz Bey did not think it necessary to reply. He just stared as if to say 'Oh, please!' He took a gulp of his rakı. He crossed his legs and sat slumped in his chair. It was as though he was the twenty-five year old Aziz Bey was taking the world in his palm and preparing to squeeze the juice out of it.

Within half an hour the tavern was filled to overflowing. Aziz Bey had taken his place among the players, and had given a long tambur taqsim. Zeki's eyes were on Aziz Bey. It was going well for the moment. He hoped that this long illness had been good for old musician. Perhaps he would be the old Aziz Bey and understand from the patrons' gaze what they liked, and would turn the night into a festivity for everyone.

But the programme began again with sad songs.

> My heart is sad again, I remembered you deep inside.
> I passed yesterday again through the old autumn gardens.

Zeki strove to keep his cool, reminding himself that it was customary for the first hour to pass with such heavy, moving songs.

The young group made up of old school friends were enough of a crowd to book the whole tavern, and they were in very good spirits. There was non-stop movement at the tables. These youngsters, who hadn't seen one other for a long time, had begun earning a living four to five years earlier and considered themselves to be successfully passing life's difficult exams. They were talking and laughing continually about those carefree, irresponsible, happy days of school with longing; mistaken by their youthful perception of time, they were talking about the days, not too distant, that they felt long gone; and they were embracing and kissing.

As the night wore on, their nostalgia slaked, their common memories were exhausted and they became slightly tipsy. The to-ing and fro-ing among the tables had diminished, and now some of them had succumbed to a fresh drunkenness, while others reached the point of looking for merry-making. Yet there was absolutely no change in Aziz Bey's programme. The music was too incomprehensible and sorrowful to respond to the enthusiasm in their souls.

While Aziz Bey sang the darkest songs of his own melancholy internal world, outside it was pouring with rain.

At the first interval Zeki felt the patrons were not happy, and he went over to Aziz Bey.

'For goodness' sake, abi,' he said, 'They're are too young to appreciate your beautiful songs. 'Please, give them whatever they want...'

Aziz Bey interrupted Zeki harshly. The shadows that descended on his face in the dim tavern had sharpened his features even more, making him look taller and thinner.

'If they can't appreciate it, what the hell are they doing here? Can't they go somewhere else?..'

He went and took his place on the stage and continued from where he'd left off with the same mournful notes and moving melodies. Zeki's nerves were really tense. He caught Bahri's eye and said, 'Cheerful! Cheerful!' But Bahri hung his head as if to say there was nothing he could do. Zeki's face grew sour. His jaw was hurting from gritting his teeth. Aziz Bey had immediately descended to, and was now wandering about in, the depths of his own world. Even though Bahri and Mercan occasionally tried to start a cheerful song, Aziz Bey's sharp glance and the sound of his tambur virtually enveloped the whole room and wouldn't allow it.

Two smooth-shaven young men in shirts with cufflinks, imbued with the air of banks, corporations, the stock exchange, securities and real estate, had removed their jackets and loosened their ties, had put their heads together and asked everyone, laughing all the while, to write their requests on a table napkin. They tucked in a fair amount of money, and handed this to Davut. After handing over the requests, one could tell from the way they sprawled in their chairs and the superior look on their faces, that they were prepared to pay for the entertainment they were expecting; an insolence that said, 'That's enough, the time has come, now let's see you entertain us.' They spoke incessantly and teased their girl friends at tables further off. They did not like the mezes and sent them back, then sent the busboys running to buy roses and scatter them impudently in front of the girls.

Aziz Bey saw the insolence with which these two had held out the money and the table napkin to Davut. Zeki called out 'Give it to Bahri!' but he could not make his voice heard in the general hum. Davut took the table napkin and instead of taking it to Bahri, knowing full well that this list of requests would drive Aziz Bey mad, he put it on the coffee table in front of him next to his glass.

Aziz Bey stared for a while at the table napkin with the money clearly sticking out of the corner. He finished his song. He put down his tambur and laid it beside him with care. Then he took the napkin and the money and went to the head of the long table. All the members of the group were looking at Aziz Bey with smiling faces and were hoping that this musician would play some simple joke on them. The two young men looked at each other. They were ready to make fun of this ridiculously dressed man. Zeki trembled for a moment. Davut was leaning against the wall, smirking as he waited for what was about to happen. Aziz Bey flung the money on the table, held up the table napkin like a dirty handkerchief and waved it.

'Who asked for these?' he asked in a powerful voice.

Bahri, as if sensing the disaster that was about to happen, played his clarinet with all his might, trying to stifle the situation and to cover Aziz Bey's words and the probable insults they contained. Mercan was beating his darbuka non-stop. The violinist who had newly joined the team unconsciously participated in Bahri and Mercan's efforts; as he scraped his bow across the strings a squeaky, scratchy noise came out. There was neither rhythm, nor melody, nor anything else left on the scene. Bahri realised this cacophony would only inflame Aziz Bey all the more and he put down the clarinet, Mercan's beatings on the darbuka slowed, then stopped altogether. Aziz Bey's insolent and angry mien, his eyes that looked as though they were burning under the dim light, confused the group.

There was silence. Aziz Bey's question reverberated in this silence.

'I said, who asked for these!'

He tore the table napkin into shreds and left it like confetti on the table. The pieces of the napkin fell quietly into the half-eaten beans in oil, the yogurt and garlic spread, and the salad. A half-drunk and extremely derisive voice was heard from one of the young men who'd sent the napkin.

'Are you crazy or something, uncle...'

Aziz Bey struck his fist on the table at these words and Zeki jumped on him almost simultaneously. The glasses and bottles on the wobbly table where Aziz Bey had brought his fist down promptly all fell over. When the girls saw the red wine spilling on them they screamed and cried.

Zeki began to shake Aziz Bey as he held him by the shoulder.

'Enough, you bugger! I've had enough!'

The anger that had been building up inside him for months had turned into a delicious pleasure. The words that had been ringing inside his brain for days emerged in the flavour of syrup; even he himself couldn't believe this pleasure; he took deep powerful breaths and scattered spittle from his mouth as he shouted. He hauled Aziz Bey, who had no idea what was happening to him, over to the door opened a short while ago to let out the smoke.

'I've had enough!' he shouted, 'I've had it up to here! You've ruined me! You've bankrupted me, you bastard, you've bankrupted me, you animal! Was it because I treated you kindly? Was it because I fed you, you hungry dog?'

He was hitting and shoving Aziz Bey on the shoulders with both hands at once; as he shoved, Aziz Bey staggered backwards with tiny steps, while on his face there was an expression like a child who has been unjustly rebuked.

This scene greatly offended Bahri. There was such a subdued, such an innocent expression on Aziz Bey's face that even those who witnessed the event thought that the scene that had taken place a little earlier was not real but had been a dream; they just looked undecided about what was dream and what was reality. Within seconds, Bahri came up to them while all this was happening and tried to stop Zeki.

Aziz Bey was looking with an empty expression, uncomprehending as to why Zeki had done all this, as if he had been woken up by a violent prod while sleeping quietly where he was curled up. Then he realised not the reason of the event but the action itself. He stopped, an expression as though he were about to spit passed over his face momentarily. Then that bewildered child's face hardened. A squat dwarf, a poor wretch, a piece of shit was kicking Aziz Bey around, the famous tambur player, who had grown up with music, in front of whom soloists stood to attention. His shoulders became erect in an instant. He rushed forward to give this wretch his deserts, to grind him into the dust. He raised his hand covered with age spots and got ready to hit Zeki in the face. Zeki saw this movement, the blood went to his brain, and he managed to catch not the arm moving in the air but the sleeve of the old costume whose stitches had come apart in places. He was so angry. First he pulled Aziz Bey violently towards him and then with a violent shove pushed him out of the door.

As Aziz Bey, who still thought of himself as the tall, muscular, strong, dignified young man of years before was rolling in the pool of muddy water in front of the tavern, the sleeve that had ripped from end to end of his costume remained in Zeki's hand. Bahri stopped Zeki, who was still taking great noisy breaths; caught up in the pleasure of this suddenly exploding rage. Bahri prevented Zeki from beating up the man with the sad eyes like a wet kitten in the muddy puddle. The good girls from families who believed a knife fight to be common in such places had paled, and now gathered behind Zeki ready to scream hysterically and faint if they saw a speck of blood. Everyone was stunned.

Zeki shouted in a voice hoarse with rage.

'Get out, you bastard! And never come round here again!'

Aziz Bey got up on his knees under the rain, and opening his right hand like the foot of a bird about to die, held it in the air.

'Give me my sleeve...' he moaned.

Unaware of the deep pain that he would suffer in the coming days for having caused this pathetic scene, Zeki flung the sleeve, now little more than a rag, angrily at Aziz Bey. It fell into the water. Aziz Bey took it from the water and shook it. Bahri was pulling Zeki inside as if tongue-tied, unable to say a word, but with shaking hands, Mercan was trying to see what was going on over the girls who had gathered in the doorway; Davut was smirking behind the window that covered the façade of the tavern from end to end.

Zeki stopped, took a breath and spat fiercely at Aziz Bey as he tried to get up from the water. Then he gave a violent kick to the door that was closing slowly with a crying squeal as if wanting to wipe out this image from everybody's mind and restart the film. The glass in the door, which was covered with a hand knitted curtain, came down with a crash on Aziz Bey. Zeki became limp and helpless at the sound of this rattling, eerie noise that descended on a troubled life, restless like a handful of mercury. He sat down at a table, and with shaking hands he drank the water in the first glass he could find. The patrons cowered in silence.

Aziz Bey shook off the broken glass that had fallen on him. At that moment he remembered the glass that fell out of the door that he'd slammed with rage when starting out on his long and hopeful journey. He had come to the end of a long adventure that began with a broken pane.

Bahri opened the door and went out. It was raining in torrents, individual drops almost distinguishable in the beam of the streetlight that cast a modestly murky light on this narrow, stifling street. He saw Aziz Bey walking away. His right arm covered by his white shirt slowly faded into the distance, a sad white spot in the darkness of the night, as the suit sleeve at the end of this hand trailed on the ground.

TALES OF WOMANISING

I was either going to die or be reborn from my old wounds. Women were my old wounds. Non-existent women. My decay, my life withering unbidden like a sheaf of grass; they were like rocks worn away by my worthlessness, flowing like running water.

My cowardice, my cringing, my introversion.

And then my beardlessness, the reason my wife cut my hair when it grew.

My old wounds were the layers of cardboard I lined my shoes with, and the ones I replaced as they were wore out... Sundays at home... in secret.

They were my wife's large, but scary, black eyes that made one want to cry, and her bones bulging under her knuckles.

They were the prints of red lips marking the coffee cups I carried in hands trembling with fear in my early youth when I was a merchant tailor's apprentice.

And they were my weird and wretched wedding photograph shot by the drunkard who ran the photographer's shop in the neighbourhood. We both looked as though we were crying.

But despite all this, I wouldn't have wanted my end to be like this. I had no idea. A little before the tale that I am about to relate took place I was: between the ages of thirty and forty, between being married and being single, between being alive and being dead. My life resembled a straight, long, thin line. Something like a sick person's endless moment of death. As if I'd been condemned to walk this long, thin line till eternity.

Sometimes, seemingly always in winter in the late afternoon, I'd sit at the window end of my shop counter, stare out and ask myself, *Am I a happy man?* I had a passable shop, a passable wife, a roof over my head, a meal on the hob and two children. *So I should be happy,* I'd murmur to myself.

And so I really thought, but I'd then catch a glimpse of the mirror opposite. I'd see a literally blue man, a face creased and shrunk like a cheap blue skirt lining. It was as though blue ink filled the lines of my face. My posture resembled an abandoned pet dog. For no reason I'd take down bunches of zips from the shelf, and swap the button boxes quite pointlessly. I'd attempt to sweep up the shop, and try to forget the abandoned, blue pet dog I saw in the mirror.

And that's why I abandoned myself to this strange game, like rolling very gently down a mound of sand lapped at the bottom by the waves of a warm sea.

The game started after I met Turcan. Before him, a quiet old Jew sold stockings for varicose veins in the shop next door. If we met in the mornings he'd say, *Hello neighbour,* enter his shop and leave quietly in the evenings. One day he quietly died. Turcan bought the Jew's shop. So quietness died too. If it had been up to me, when I met this man who covered his bald pate with a small chestnut wig and who, with every step he took, left an acrid, tobacco-like smell in the street, I'd wish him a dry good luck and defer introductions.

But that's not what happened. One day a small lorry drew up to the door, and as mirrors of different sizes were being unloaded an altercation began between Turcan and the porters. He dismissed the porters who'd already unloaded half of the mirrors, and sticking his head into my shop – without a by-your-leave, as if we'd been friends for forty years, and with a funny expression in his large grey-blue eyes, astounding and even frightening me, he cheerfully asked me, *Gi's a hand, neighbour?* I couldn't say a thing; there was the sourness of a lemon in my mouth: as if the words would come out shrivelled were I to speak. I came out of my shop, humped the mirrors on my back and carried them into his.

That day he took me to lunch, which led on to his tales of womanising. We drank rakı, and ate bean salad and pickled bonito. Turcan invariably talked about women. And I noticed that it was as though all the women he described were virtually boneless. I thought about those women's hands, and my eyes were dazzled by the whiteness of their skin. And then how talkative and warm the women he talked about were. They knew how to laugh.

And that's the least of it. Women kept calling Turcan on his mobile. He exchanged smutty banter, roared with laughter and belched every now and then. His forehead sweated as he laughed, and when he wiped it away his wig moved. While he was speaking to women, to the women I imagined to be virtually boneless and so very pale, I thought how very many and beautiful women there were in the world. My wife never once came to my mind while thinking about the beautiful women in the world. My old wounds hurt. My rib cage felt as though it had collapsed after a huge punch, too tight for the trouble within me; all those tales of womanising infested my insides like a deep and fatal affliction.

A few days later, Turcan introduced me to two of his friends and took me out to dinner. Tales of womanising multiplied and became more varied. They three tall men received calls from women non-stop, as sat with their coats over their shoulders and spoke of cheques, maturity dates, and of course, women. I listened to them and laughed too late, struggled to understand. Late in the evening, they got up to meet go and meet the women they'd been talking about; I assumed a knowing smile and nodded meaningfully. They wouldn't let me pay the bill. With avuncular smiles, they patted me on the shoulder.

A coy snow fell as we left the restaurant. I said goodbye to them with a cordiality I'd never before shown, and as the three men raffishly got into the car brought from the car park, I said I'd take a cab and beckoned to a taxi. I opened the door of the taxi that stopped and waved to them before I got in. Their car passed under the street lights of the road now totally devoid of its daytime crowds, and, disappeared noisily like their guffaws. Turning to the taxi driver, I told him I'd left something in the inside and asked him to wait. Then I closed the taxi door and walked back towards the restaurant, but turned instead into a street and listened. I heard the driver wait for a while, then accelerate away in a rage, skidding on the empty road and screeching all the way. I came out of hiding and began to walk. The layers of cardboard I'd lined my shoes with had worn thin, my rib cage caved in, and I felt that my face growing bitter; yet I told myself, *It's from the snow, it's from the wind.*

I turned into my street, to the dejected waving of the poor, threadbare washing on the lines stretched between the buildings. The lights of the street lamps changed from blue to orange, reflected in the dark windows of the neighbourhood that had long since gone to bed. As I approached home a strange joy grew within me. It was in front of my front door I took the first step into this game that was to bring me to a tragic end. An erectness sprung to my shoulders, as though I had grown taller. I stroked my non-existent beard with my hands blue with cold, and, despite having a key and knowing full well that the door buzzer was broken, I pressed the bell button by then entrance. Then I raised my head and looked up. Whether the lights in my flat were on or not, I cannot remember. This was because I looked, but I did not see; women of all types passed in front of my eyes. That is why I didn't notice the anxiety (that I recalled much later) on the face of my wife who'd put on a cardigan over her flannel nightdress and come down five flights of stairs in a fluster.

That night I know that I kept smiling as I slept.

I had five nights like that. Five nights in short intervals... But each was more disagreeable than the previous; each time Turcan and his friends took less interest in me than on the previous one. At the end of the fifth night, they forgot me in the toilet. I was a handful of ashes they had blown away and scattered.

The sixth night never came because they didn't invite me again. But I continued these nights on my own.

Why did I play this game, and for whom? I don't know. But I enjoyed playing it while I did, I was happy. That's all. Would I ever have played it if I'd known it would turn out like this?

When I realised a sixth night wasn't going to happen, I asked myself three questions.

One: Was it anxiety I saw on my wife's face – my wife who

came down five floors to open the door for me at the end of these five nights?

Two: I've a faint recollection of it being warm inside when I arrived home. Was it the alcohol that kept away the cold, or was my home warm because my wife had waited for me the whole night, and had thrown coal into the stove while waiting?

Three: In the early hours of the morning of these nights, in the moments when I was about to pass into sleep from fantasies full of tales of womanising, in the dark I'd feel my wife's eyes staring at my face, and her short nailed, bony fingers whose tips burnt like fire wiping the sweat from my brow. At these times, I used to think I was dreaming. Furthermore, those bony fingers that entered my fantasies of beautiful women and angered me, and for that reason I used to have an uneasy sleep. Was this feeling the result of a dream or were those bony fingers real?

Then I pondered. I found the answers to my questions.

One: At the end of these five nights my wife *was* anxious each time I arrived home. I remember she whispered hurt, agitated words about her concern for me, and that I looked at her angrily with my bloodshot eyes and gave no answer.

Two: During these five nights the stove had always been burning; in other words, my wife had waited up. Because when I got up in the mornings heavy-eyed I'd find the dying embers of a large piece of coal that had been thrown into the stove at some late hour.

Three: I was angry at those fingers that wiped the sweat from my brow, with that bony but caring touch, because they were not the things I desired. But after harshly pushing away the fingers whose tips burnt like embers, I'd also hear a suppressed sob dissolve and disappear in a weak and tired body.

And that's why I began the sixth-night game.

I was sitting in my shop, in my own silence. From next door came the sound of Turcan's heels and female laughter reminiscent of the tinkling of cut glass. I imagined there was a crowd of women with Turcan. Virtually boneless, with sparkling complexions, chatty, lively women... Then evening fell, the lights from the chemist, the second-hand bookseller and the kiosk opposite came on one by one, reflected in the puddles of the cobbled street. The city's tired and stooped people hastened their steps. I forgot to put on the lights. The women must have started to leave Turcan's shop; because I smelt vanilla, lilac, lemon blossom and coconut. I closed my eyes tightly and sank into these strange, scented, invisible clouds. In the street the sounds abated, as the shops all closed. The rubbish from the stores and houses was piled up in the middle of the street. Then the sounds outside changed. They turned into vulgar yells, curses, screams, police sirens and the sound of running feet. Night fell, night progressed.

I got up from where I had sat all day; I wound my scarf around my neck, put on my coat, and my cap that was too small for my misshapen head; I closed the shop and pulled down the metal shutters; I began to walk slowly. I walked up and down the road, how many times? I don't remember. Then I entered a poky, cheap tavern, down four steps in one of the back streets. I drank half a small bottle of rakı in small sips, taking my time. I looked at my watch; it was much too early. While drinking my rakı my eyes kept filling with tears, I wiped them with the back of my hand; to those around I was pretending I'd got cigarette smoke in my eyes.

I left the tavern and again walked up and down the length of the road. I got cold, and I passed in front of the taverns where groups of men and women were singing together. I looked at the neon lights of the cheap nightclubs from a distance, but I didn't get near enough any to see the photographs of the dancers in the glass panels hanging by the doors. There were police cars parked in the middle of the road and glue-sniffing children tumbled about in front of me. I heard the screeches of cats and hearty curses of women past their prime assailed my ears. The road that I was walking along ended and I began again; it finished, I walked again.

My shoes got wet and I was cold. I had no choice but return to the shop, but after first buying a bottle of wine from the corner off-licence. I opened the shutters softly, but my hands shook as

I turned the lock. I sneaked into my shop like a thief, and didn't turn on the lights. I went to the counter and sat on my stool. I was confused, and in a strange way I was excited; I was exhausted from the strain of pretending something that wasn't happening was happening, and that's why I forgot to turn on the electric fire.

Suddenly I felt like crying. I leant my head on my arms and fell asleep crying.

When I woke up my back was like ice; I turned on the small light on the counter and looked at the clock; for the sixth night running, it was a good time to return home. I took a couple of large swigs from the wine bottle, replaced the cork and hid the bottle under the counter. I sneaked out of my shop again and went home.

This time too, those three questions continually to bother me, and this time, I looked up at the windows of my flat from below. I was maudlin. I wanted to hug my wife, to bury my face in her shoulder, to say, *I haven't been anywhere tonight...* I felt her protruding shoulder blades under my hands. Then I remembered her ribs and the bones that bulged from her fingers, the dullness, the lifelessness of her yellowish, swarthy face. The windows changed colour with the rays of the television that was on. The bony woman had not slept.

And so that anger, that anger that had dragged me into this meaningless game suddenly grew inside me. It was unfair, I know... But it happened. I rang the bell longer and with more rage than previously. I didn't look at the face of my wife who virtually raced down the stairs with flustered steps. I was afraid that those fantasies of sweet hued women, boneless women, with faces reminiscent of twittering birds which had entered my dreams in the shop as I went to sleep crying, would be spoiled. I heard my wife murmuring a question in her peeved, hurt voice. Shut it! I said harshly. I lay down on the bed in my clothes and closed my eyes.

In actual fact, I didn't fall asleep, but lay fully conscious. But a drunken snore came from my mouth. I heard my wife sobbing a tiny, frail sound; I felt a broad smile spread over my face, a smile that I wasn't in control of. I was lying on my back, but it was as if the panes of the window at the foot of my bed had risen to the ceiling, and with my open eyes I saw my face in these panes that covered the room's ceiling. In the light from the moonlight that filtered into the room, the smile on my face resembled a gaping, bleeding wound. I thought I was having a nightmare.

On the seventh night I didn't visit the same tavern. I had no money to spend there. I bought cheese, pickles, and dried fruit and nuts. I spread them all out on the counter on a sheet of newspaper. And I drank the rest of the wine. Every now and then I turned off the electric fire to save money. I put my coat over my shoulders and fell asleep again. This time I didn't cry; I went further with the women in my dreams. Again I returned home towards morning. Again I rang the bell from below. This time, I didn't just tear a strip off my wife, but I also pushed her roughly by the shoulders. When I got up in the morning I realised she wasn't speaking to me. I laughed to myself. But she still had to make herself ask for money for the market, to buy the lad some shoes. She wasn't talking to me, but she still had to ask for money. I left it like flinging it in front of her.

A few days later, a stout woman with perspiration on her upper lip came into the shop. She bought a whole load of things; lining, interfacing, binding, buttons, a zip and I don't know what else. She was in a hurry, in a fluster, and she was chatty. As she left she forgot her bag, but I didn't say a word. As soon as she went out, I rummaged through the contents. Somehow I managed to quickly take the lipstick out of her bag, throw it in the till, then come running out of the shop with the bag in my hand, shouting, *Madame, you've forgotten your bag!* I don't know quite how; I did it in a jiffy. After hastily checking her bag she thanked me profusely. My heart was pounding in case she realised the lipstick wasn't there, but she noticed I'd pinched it. I smiled at her with an honest, decent face and then I watched her mingling with the crowd, swaying her heavy hips from right to left, happy she'd escaped lightly from this little mishap. The people of the city were flowing from the streets to the road and it was crowded. Watching them, even for a few seconds, enervated me and I returned to my shop. I was amazed that my hands were trembling so much as I took the lipstick out of the till drawer; they actually burnt as though I had grasped a glowing ember. My palm sweated. I put the lipstick down, wiped my palms on my trousers and took it in my hand again.

That night I went home, went to bed early and heard my wife saying to the children, *Be quiet, your father's tired, he's sleeping.* All the while, I kept thinking about that lipstick. The blood-like red, its gliding texture...

The following night I ate my dinner in the shop and drank my wine. I phoned home and heard my wife saying, *Hello! hello!* in her excited and frightened voice; I put the phone down without saying anything.

Later on, this was something that I did this frequently. Luckily for me, I'd answered a few wrong numbers while at home, and insisted that's what they were a little too forcefully. My wife had stared at me with her sorrowful eyes and had gone to bed early.

For a while I read the usual magazines that my neighbour, the second-hand bookseller, was forced to take from his important customers, despite not being able to sell them. He used to wrap up parcels and give them out here and there to people like me. It was pouring. I heard it beating on the half-open shutters. It was as though the rain was covering up something that I was secretly doing, it was concealing and smothering it with a din. The lipstick was on the counter. I got undressed and took off my shirt. I applied the lipstick to my lips and transferred lipstick print onto my shirt collar, and even dabbed a little against the edge of my vest, too.

I stared at the mark on my shirt for such a long time, and during that time so many and such a variety of women passed through my mind, that I stood in a trance for such a long time and got cold. Collecting myself hastily, I got dressed. Just as I was about to leave the mirror caught my eye. I saw the face of a pathetic man in the mirror, blue of face, wearing red lipstick and I recoiled. I wiped my lips with a paper napkin. I rubbed the paper napkin so hard on my lips that they turned red and looked as though they still had lipstick on. I sat for a while and waited for the redness to pass.

I learned much later that my wife, who noticed the spot of lipstick the next morning, had cried all day.

Meanwhile time passed. A few days of the week I went home on time. On others I listened to the radio in the shop and built castles in the air. I enjoyed my wife wandering around me with a sulky face, her looking at me with beseeching eyes; I felt her crying secretly, and I smiled. I heard her moaning as though she'd fallen into the clutches of some terrible illness. I can't guess how long all this lasted. However, with every passing day I enjoyed this game even more. Now I too had a tale of womanising, and the only one who believed in it was my wife.

By now my frail, unattractive, bony wife was growing thinner every day. Her large eyes had for a long time been veiled in tears, and stared with a deep sorrow, evoking not beauty, but the desire to cry. I was trying to write the end to a non-existent tale of womanising, and even forgetting to caress my children.

I bought a red tie with little blue hearts on it from a salesman who came to the shop one late afternoon. He said he worked on ships and swore he'd brought this tie in Europe. I didn't believe that he'd even seen a seaside city other than Istanbul. I took it anyway and put it on over my garish, dark-brown wool shirt. I knew it didn't go very well, but I didn't mind a bit. There was a strange joy inside me, as if I hadn't bought the tie with my own hands, but, like an unexpected gift, found it suddenly in the palm of my hand.

I turned on the radio, and while wondering whether the girl presenter who was saying, *Tell your loved one you love her at every opportunity,* was blonde or brunette, a whole lot of customers suddenly descended. I treated them each cheerfully, not even getting angry with those who made me bring down the boxes near the ceiling, open bolts of lining material, and left without buying anything. I didn't tell Mukadder *abla*, the dressmaker's apprentice, that her debts had accumulated.

Then I closed my shop when everyone else did, and wandered the night about the streets with the tie round my neck. When I returned to the shop again later, I opened a tin of fried aubergines and drank two bottles of beer. Then I went home. I saw my wife's eyes, that had for some time been continually tearful, were fixed on my tie, and that she suddenly drooped as if the blood drained from her. She went to bed without saying a word to me. The following morning, I saw that contrary to her usual habit, she hadn't hung my shirt and trousers, but just left them there; and she hadn't touched the tie. While I was getting dressed I watched her from the corner of my eye; she avoided turning her face towards me as I did up my tie at length, busying herself with something or other, and shouting at the children for no reason. I smiled.

Strangely, although all this convinced my wife I had a mistress, it wasn't enough for me. And now, after all that's happened, I wonder whether the man who came that day to the shop, gave a bulk order and paid for it all on the spot, and whom I thought was such good luck for me, was actually part of my wife's dark destiny.

The days had lengthened, spring had arrived and a few shoots had even sprouted from the tree stump that had been crushed by hundreds of heavy wheels in the street. In spite of spring my wife was desperately unhappy.

It was early in the morning, and while the kiosk man had yet to skewer his *döner* on the spit, and the lazy second-hand bookseller to open his shop, an elderly man with sweaty hands came in. He had retired, he was going to open a shop for his wife and he had ready cash. If we could come to an agreement, he was going to buy a heap of things. He wondered whether I could be of help to him. He was a strange customer, a little naïve, and clearly had no clue about business. We bargained until midday. I made the greatest sale of my life. I sold a huge amount of goods to the man who was going to open a shop for his wife who was bored at home. He paid half immediately and wrote a cheque for the remainder. Suddenly, I had a lot of money. I was so glad and cheerful, yet towards evening this large sum began to frighten me. I decided I couldn't stay in the shop. As soon as I put the money in my pocket, I left.

I went to one of the nightclubs I'd always stared at from a distance, but never had the courage to enter. The money in my pocket had intoxicated me. The bouncers at the door laughed and said, *It's much too early. Come towards midnight.* I didn't know what to do. I thought briefly of going back to sit in the shop, but I didn't feel like it. Spring had come, you see. There was the smell of pollen in the air. I was fed up of just sitting quietly in the dark, behind closed shutters.

So I went to a tavern. As I entered I checked my pocket. My money was in its place. But I couldn't drink; I was frightened that I'd get drunk and get robbed. And just in case they thought I wasn't drinking because I was skint, I ordered a whole lot of mezes. I ordered broad beans in yoghurt, for instance, and artichokes, things I hadn't had for years. I ordered a mixed grill and then ordered another. I surreptitiously spilled the rakı on the floor. I kept looking at my watch but it was only nine, so I decided to go to the cinema. I stared hungrily at the naked women in the film, and when it finished time had come. I didn't go to the same nightclub, but went to another one.

It was strange, it was as if they knew I had money; at the door they showed me every respect. I went inside and sat at a table. My tie was round my neck. I was very excited as this was my first time, but I was afraid too. I was trying to conceal my fear. A woman came and wanted to sit at my table and I felt myself stammering and sweating. I took all I had to say, *Of course, do sit down.* Then she began to pester me. She was pale, just as I'd imagined, but she spoke incessantly and I couldn't hear what she was saying because of the noise. I started staring at her mouth opening and closing, and notices she had a rotten tooth that stank. Then my eyes fixed on her sweaty, flabby armpits; the pale woman's light blue dress with the overgenerous décolleté had gone pitch-black at the armpits. She carried on drinking, and so did I.

As I drank I relaxed, I became clearer. First I talked about this and that and at one point, with the excuse of getting the waiter to fetch some cigarettes, I flashed my money. Then a certain courage came over me. I became tall and straight-shouldered. I said to her,

'There is just one thing I want from you. Whatever it costs, I'll pay you.'

She thought I wanted to sleep with her, and as she looked me over and I saw her lip curl up mockingly; my blood drained, my old wound, my old fear retuned, never letting me go...

'Just say the word, big boy,' she said, 'But I'm expensive. Just so you know.'

My eyes sought the smarmy photographer who was wandering around, capturing the ever-changing women's faces under the colourful lights with a flash of his camera.

'Let's have a photo together,' I said, 'but a proper intimate one. Gaze at me like you love me.'

She laughed for so long I clenched my fists.

'Don't even mention it, big boy. Just give the money and then see how I love you.'

Then, before I could say another word, she called out to the photographer, drew close to me, put her head on my chest and an arm around my waist. I was bewildered, as though it wasn't me who'd proposed it in the first place. I didn't know where to put my hand. The photographer said,

'Hug her back, abi; you're as stiff as a board.'

He held my head and turned it to the woman and put my arm on her bare, greasy shoulder.

'Gaze into *abla*'s eyes. For heaven's sake smile a little, abi!'

The flash went, again and again. I noticed the woman was really enjoying herself. She'd joined forces with the photographer, and the two were shoving me into various poses. She pressed her cheek to my cheek, she kissed me, and then while she was rubbing off the trace of lipstick, she smiled at the photographer and we entwined our arms and drank. Then she got bored. And told him to push off.

Towards morning, the photographer deposited a stack of photographs on the table. She chose one from amongst them and suggested she write on the back. Clicking her fingers she summoned the waiter,

'Gi's a pen,' she said.

The fingers that asked for a pen quivered in the air, waited in agitation. The waiter handed her the same pen with which he'd written the bill, and wanting to join in the fun, leant his thigh against the table, rested his hand on his waist and began to watch. She bit the top of the pen and then asked,

'What's your name, big boy?'

'Why do you ask?' I said.

'Gonna write it, aren't we?'

'Never mind my name,' I replied.

'Well, what we gonna write then?' she asked.

This strange request of mine must have made the rounds around the nightclub staff in no time at all, because the waiter chipped in and told her to write *To my greatest love*.

'Hey mate, that's good, bravo!' she replied, .

And all this time, I was just staring. Bewildered and shrunk... She wrote, *A lifeless memento, to my greatest love*. Then she turned to me,

'What should my name be?' she asked.

'What?'

'What is your name?'

'It says Cansev on the poster, but I'll be whoever you want, love,' she replied, 'What should I write on the back of the photo?'

'Cansev will do,' I said, 'that's fine.'

'Sure thing, whatever you want it shall be, big boy, he who pays the piper calls the tune.'

She wrote Cansev, and signed it. Then she giggled,

'Wait, let me look at those again,' she said

Looking at the pictures one by one, she ripped up the one or two she didn't like,

'I haven't come out well. Who're you going to fool with these, big boy? Show off to your friends?'

I gave no answer. She smiled a little as though she pitied me and then got tired of waiting, and with an, *Eeeh, none of my bleeding business!* she got up. She was swaying, barely able to stand on her feet. Her face grew serious as though the fun was over and the cinema crowd had dispersed. She stretched out her hand with short stubby fingers and long nails painted the colour of dried blood,

'Pay up and let's go.'

When I left the cheap nightclub my cash was considerably diminished, but I had a whole lot of photographs in my jacket pocket, and signed, too. I went to the shop and made a lot of noise as I parted the shutters. I entered, sat on the counter and stared at the photos one by one; I read the woman's scrawly writing and smiled. Then I removed the thin cardboard covers on the photos with the name of the nightclub and tore them up. I put the signed photograph in my pocket and spread the others over the counter. As day broke I went home. I rang the bell from downstairs. I realised my wife's footsteps were no longer agitated and timid sounds, but that she walked as though she were dragging her feet. She didn't look at my eyes, and after opening the door she went upstairs again with tired, weary steps, and we went to bed without speaking.

The next morning I deliberately didn't wear that jacket; using spring as an excuse to go out in shirtsleeves and walk to the shop. Then in the evening I saw that my wife was very subdued. She was quiet, it was though she didn't see me; she wasn't even sulking and her behaviour was very strange. She took no notice of the children's noise. In the morning the boy came to me and told me they were going to their uncles for the day, and I gave him my approval without really paying attention.

*

That day I was uneasy; I spread out the photos I'd looked at a hundred times again on the counter, and waited for Turcan. He didn't appear; his assistant looked after the shop. In the evening I went to a shop that sold mezes, I was planning to drink in the shop again but then suddenly I decided not to. My feet dragged me home.

It was crowded in front of my door. A police car stood there, blue and red lights flashing, and an ambulance. I approached rather puzzled; the sun had set, the streetlights had come on and the revolving lights of the police car and the ambulance reflected in the windows. There was a stir, and when the opposite neighbour saw me she called to the police, *Her husband's here! Her husband's here!*

I felt dizzy, and can't really remember what happened next. Through the door they brought out a black bag on a stretcher, which they loaded into the ambulance. They wouldn't let me go home. When I went home a few days later I saw the cracks in the plaster surrounding the chandelier hook in the ceiling. My wife had hanged herself. With a clothesline. Left the children with her elder brother. The way she just swung on the rope reflected in the window of the flat opposite each time the sun shone. It had attracted the attention of the people on the top floor. On the dining table had been the red tie with blue hearts and my photo with Cansev. The police had taken the lot.

My wife was a bony woman.

No, she wasn't beautiful, but she had a heart.

I never knew.

A COLD WINTER

Despite putting on many layers of clothes and laying his old overcoat on top of two mouldy quilts and a blanket riddled with moth holes, Semavi Bey had been unable to sleep the whole night from the cold. Yet he'd been prepared for this cold winter. In the days when autumn's mellow freshness first began to make itself felt, he'd stared at the creeper that for years had patiently spread over all the walls of his house and had suddenly, foolishly turn red, and murmured, 'This winter will be very cold...' He had started to take precautions even then.

He had taped draft excluder around all the windows of the ground floor where he lived, stuffed newspaper under the balcony doors that were rotten from damp and poked old sheets into the cracks in the wood with which he'd closed off the stairwell that led to the first floor. But in spite of all his efforts, he had been unable to stop the wind virtually roaring through the house, and the walls almost icing over. This winter was bleaker and harsher than previous ones.

To be honest, seasons held no importance for Semavi Bey. Neither the first buds of spring, nor the autumn clouds that gathered over the Bosphorus, lending its waters strange colours, moved him. But his body grew more sensitive to hot and cold as it grew older. The yellow beams of summer's sunshine warmed his insides, and winter's cold froze his bones more than they did anyone else. Since the day he felt he'd grown old, he regarded his body as a dog following him wherever he went, desperate to offer him pointless love. He quarrelled with his own body every time he became hungry, thirsty, or cold. Not that this body showed any sympathy for his wretched soul dried up from years of suffering.

Now, with his eyes half open, he listened to his body as it

continued to shiver. Taking his arm out from under the quilt that exuded an oppressive smell of damp, he touched the eight-segment electric radiator that failed to heat itself, let alone the room, despite being on all night long. All it managed was to form a small, lukewarm area around itself. He knew these eight feeble segments wouldn't suffice all winter. Taking his arm back inside, he pulled the quilt over his head. He tried hard not to cry. Because he couldn't look at fire, he suffered terribly this way every winter, as he did every year of the life he'd frittered away like running water. He lived an unhappy and resentful life, left to the cruelty of his own destiny, a man politely driven from familiar doors for his eccentric disposition and peculiar fears. He was amazed that his body still functioned more or less in spite of the death of his spirit, and at every cell carrying on life as a faithful representative of the natural instinct of living. He had virtually numbed his mind and had banished that incident that had brought his life to an unnerving state of slavery to the most secret corner of his memory. As long as he did not look at fire, his spirit could be as peaceful as a calm sea. But this inability to look at fire turned winters into terrible torture for him. All because of fire.

He lifted the quilt and stared at the light filtering into his room through the magnificent creeper that, having completely enveloped his bedroom window, had climbed to the balcony of the first floor, a great part of which had burnt years ago. Because it had never been touched again, it had turned into a mound of black ashes and a tip full of memories,

Such a long time to go before winter ends, he thought to himself. The snow had stopped for the moment. The rays of a deceptive winter sun were filling the room in lines, and the shadows of leaves were playing on his face. He closed his eyes tight, utterly miserable.

He thought how this fraudulent sun that scattered small, false crumbs of hope within him would soon vanish between the clouds, and the skies would suddenly darken, making his wounded spirit ache once again. All day long he'd wander about warm places where he wouldn't see fire, drinking something hot in an effort to comfort this body that refused to warm up unless the golden rays of the sun were visible. Then, at the hour when everyone withdrew home, he would return to this splendid ruin, bemoaning the fact that he'd pass the night to come shivering again under mouldy quilts.

The coldness of the walls that had at one time been adorned with expensive paintings and gilt mirrors was almost palpable on his own skin. He felt so cold. He must leave the house immediately and go to the coffeehouse where he had his daily breakfast of tea and a fresh bread *simit* straight out of the oven; he must sit with his back to the stove and, staring at the dirty foamy waters of the Bosphorus, he must sit until he warmed up his bones, pursuing the numerous thoughts that went through his mind. And then he must use up the remaining hours of a day here and there.

He put on his clothes over his pyjamas. When he came to the door, he checked his key, turned and glanced back at the house. The house was like a rotting body. He took an insatiable delight in the groaning deterioration of this place that his father had given a lifetime to build and furnish. The sad state of this house, that was the signature of a life spent with despotism, cruelty, and rage. It seemed to be a revenge for his wasted life. He stood for a moment at the door. It was as though the damp patches had perked up, as though one more rusty wire had snapped from inside the wireless, as though the mould that had totally invaded the back rooms of the house had advanced to the drawers of the desk at which that man – always angry – put on his reading glasses and occupied himself with money matters to forget himself during the times he didn't go to the office. These sounds, that nobody else but he could hear, pacified his spirit pleasantly. He shut the door and went out. The state of the garden that his father had created, looking at pictures of English gardens and continually reprimanding the gardener, was even more tragic. The trees that he left to their own devices seemed to be in mourning: sombre and withered. Snow filled the empty, broken flowerpots. As he exited the garden, the iron gate with the broken hinge swung behind him with all the aimlessness of his life.

He felt warmer, more cheerful as he went down the icy slope. Going out was good for him. Exactly like the trees in the garden, he withered descending gloom of the house. He sat in a sagging armchair in front of the window overlooking the Bosphorus, staring at a distant spot for hours, crying, feeling cold and remembering his wife. At times he'd take his eyes off the shimmering lights of the Bosphorus, and ask himself, 'Am I mad?' He could not stand even the striking of a match or the flame of a lighter, and even the sight of a roaring stove took him to his bed, feeling ill. He knew very well the reason for all this, but never made the slightest effort to rid himself of this obsession. He was desperate and silent like a bird without wings, a blind dog, or a beached and forgotten boat. Tedious days followed one another, all very similar and all very far from any emotion.

It was only on days he ran out of cash that he cheered up. On such days, because he spent his life in one bedroom and a sitting room, he'd begin wandering around the other rooms, those he never used, and whatever there was of his father's favourite things – a spiral striped piece of glassware, a piece of Meissen porcelain, a music box, a valuable picture or a mantel clock – whatever he came across, he'd tuck under his arm and immediately make for the antique dealer and peddle it. However, those things that he could tuck under his arm and cheerfully see the back of had been exhausted; the time had come for the big pieces. Because of the valuable antiques he brought along, the antique dealer would greet him at the door and go out of his way to please him whenever he went. So now, he go out to one of the kiosks on the coast road (he had never reconnected his own phone, cut off years ago) and the antique dealer would come to the house within half an hour. No matter how many times the dealer had offered to buy the whole lot, Semavi Bey wouldn't relinquish the pleasure of selling whatever his father had valued, and selling it all piece by piece; these possessions of the man who'd poisoned his own life with his cruelty and cold heart.

And today was one of those days when he'd have to telephone the antique dealer, when a small lorry would come to the gate, and when he'd eye the objects in the house one by one, wondering with pleasure, *Which one should I sell?* While he was thinking about all this, it suddenly grew dark, and a blizzard began. He realised he must go to the coffeehouse right away. He liked this coffeehouse because the stove was far inside, and where he didn't have to see the owner open the lid, throw on coal, and watch the flames virtually swallow the black pieces of coal, lick the lid and escape outside. He went down the slope, came to the coast road and walked with purpose. The blizzard made it almost impossible to see in front of him.

He thought something was amiss only occurred to him when he had already arrived under the plane tree in front of the coffeehouse. It was closed. He approached and saw that the door had been locked and sealed. He realised the owner, who allowed gambling at nights in the inner section where the stove burned, must finally have been caught. Suddenly he felt homeless. His face became tearful like a child who's lost its mother in a large marketplace. He simply stood under the plane tree wondering where to go. Where would he warm this grumpy body, exhausted from shivering all night? And he felt so tired... He stood still, not knowing what to do. He couldn't think of anywhere to go.

A city bus rent the snowstorm that kept everyone at home, and left chain-tyre tracks on the snow-covered road as it clattered past. He began to walk, following the bus tracks. There was no one on the streets. When he saw that all the shops were closed, he realised that it was Sunday and also very early in the morning, and as always he felt very much alone in this very large city, this very large country, this very large world.

A cold, keen wind cutting his face stifled the pain that this feeling gave to his spirit. He was freezing. He gave up following the tracks of the bus and turned into a side street. He'd walked quickly and was tired. His heart, stuffed for years with a deep, morbid love and a bitter hatred, was no longer able to stand these fast walks. He sheltered under the eaves of a building when he got out of breath, leaning against the wall and almost slumping to the ground. The thought of spending the whole day looking for somewhere warm seemed impossible. He thought about his distant cousins, about how warm all their houses were... He pictured the polite embarrassment on their faces. Their looks that said, *You've sat long enough, off you go now...* The loneliness in their warm, fancy houses, where the phone rang constantly, was bitterer than the one in his rotting house. While he was thinking of those people who had walked one by one out of his silent past and who were even then cold and distant, he noticed that the dilapidated building right opposite him was a bathhouse. A 'For Men' sign written in red gloss paint was hanging on the door. He couldn't believe his eyes. He'd found somewhere he'd warm his marrow, his bones, somewhere where the delight of this warming would enrapture him.

Pushing open the door of the bathhouse cautiously, he entered. There was no one about. He stood there timidly as though he'd entered a forbidden place. He couldn't find the courage to call out, 'Is anyone there?' As he was about to lose himself in the dimness of the place and the smell of the steam and cheap soap, the bath attendant came, red-faced from the heat, and with his shirt wide open.

'Were you looking for someone, uncle?' he asked, because the likelihood of a customer arriving almost at the crack of dawn in such snowy and stormy weather was so slim. His manner may have been rough, but he meant well. Semavi Bey swallowed, and visualising the baths a few paces away, where boiling water flowed from taps into marble basins, and where hot steam rose into the air, he asked,

'I was going to take a bath. The bathhouse is open, isn't it?' Although he was used to every type of customer, this strange and timid man who'd arrived in such weather amazed the bath attendant.

'It's open, but we've only just lit the boiler,' he replied. 'It's cold inside. Go and come back in a couple of hours.'

A couple of hours? Time is relative, life is a long, dark dream. A couple of hours just flew by in the coffeehouse looking at the shimmering waters of the Bosphorus as he tried to remember one or two pleasant days in the past; but how could he while away a couple of hours when his toes were about to freeze? Suddenly he felt faint and faltered. The bath attendant grabbed Semavi Bey by the arm, and stared at this poor man who was now murmuring, 'I feel so cold...' He looked at the fine features of his unshaven face, and at the clothes that, although old, reflected the refined taste of a few generations back. Drawing up a chair, he said, 'Sit here until the bathhouse has warmed up. I'll pull the chair near the stove, if you like...'

When Semavi Bey heard the word stove he flinched. His eyes searched all around for the object in question. The colossal coal stove was smouldering in the entrance to the bathhouse, cheering up this wet place that smelt of soap. Turning his back to the stove and sitting on the chair, he looked at the bath attendant for a moment with grateful eyes. A touching smile appeared on his face, and then he turned his eyes down to the floor as though the burden of spending his life with such apprehension lay with him alone. He murmured in a voice barely audible, 'It's fine here...' He wanted to vanish, to melt away like a continually lathering piece of soap in the bathhouse. He drew his body together on the chair and hunched his back; making himself look much older than he was.

'Would you like some tea?'

He nodded shyly. The forlorn sadness and fatigue in his smile shook the bath attendant. He went to pour out the tea without knowing why this tragic scene affected him so much.

Semavi Bey sat on the same chair until the bathhouse heated up. Staring at the toes of his shoes, he quietly drank the two glasses of tea that the bath attendant brought him. When the bathhouse warmed up, he took the loincloth, clogs, bowl and soap, undressed in his room and entered the bath, which was now hot enough to soften his body, almost rigid with cold.

He was strangely happy. The bath was hot but the inside of

this body that had shivered in a room whose walls were iced over, was still frozen. He went over and sat beside a marble basin and poured bowls of hot water over his head. Somehow the shivering inside him wouldn't go away. The moment hot water touched his skin, an odd shuddering shook his whole body. At last he grew warm, everything softened, and when he had no strength left in his arm from pouring hot water over himself, he lay down on the marble slab in the centre of the bath and closed his eyes. The bath was as hot as could be; steam obscured the polygonal dome windows. He'd surrendered all his muscles, bones, and nerves, everything that made up this worn-out body and this buffeted spirit, into the hands of heat and steam. How wonderful this was. What a wonderful thing to warm up without seeing the flames that savagely swallow a young body – to feel your body virtually numb.

At some point, he'd begun to feel dizzy. So agreeable was this dizziness, that an expression of happiness no one had seen for a long time affixed itself to his countenance. The sound of the water dripping from the tap that he'd failed to turn off properly grew louder, echoing in the high-ceilinged marble place. This sound heightened his loneliness. He was on his own on a snowy day in a bathhouse, just as he had been throughout his life. Yet whatever he did, he had done to be loved. He'd believed he'd be alone if he didn't love. That's why he'd loved a great deal.

'Mother!' he moaned, 'Mother, where are you?'

He began crying plaintively like a child, while at the same time strangely enjoying this state. Like the times he'd cried for no reason in his nanny's lap, the nanny whose bosom smelt like cloves and cinnamon, strange and exceedingly oriental.

'Why do all children have mothers and I don't?' he used to ask, burying his nose in the soft neck of the dark-skinned woman. The woman, watchful of the firm footsteps of a perpetually angry man, sighed with a deep sadness in her dark, kohl-rimmed eyes, and then she'd tell him melancholy tales about beautiful women, loving but unloved. As he listened to those tales, his tiny child's mind realised that his mother, whom his father had not loved enough, had left. The more he was berated on every occasion by his father, he thought about how this harsh, cruel man was incapable of loving a woman, and he promised himself again and again that when the day came and he got to know a woman he would love her very, very much, and never let her leave him.

Now the heat of the bath seemed to him like the heat of a love that had eluded him. His heart beat as though he would suddenly see his mother. As he was trying to remember that maternal face of his childhood dream, the face of his wife floated into his mind out of the blue. His childish sobs mingled with the sound of water echoing in the steam-filled dome.

His wife was saying, 'Don't love me! I don't want you to!' holding a gas lamp, a deep pain on her beautiful face like the gash of a knife.

Yet he'd never go to sleep until she slept, and always woke up before she did; he'd gaze for hours at her face where pure beauty was united with an irresistible innocence. He was so lonely, and he so wanted to love his wife, that time just dragged by without her. He thought about her and wanted to be with her every minute. He even thought about her at the office where he went, every day. He had been incapable of finding the power to oppose his father and was constantly rebuked for his uselessness while his father showered someone with orders on the telephone in his angry, deep voice. Even there, he thought about his wife with a simple smile on his face: he was happy that he could love someone.

His wife was the daughter of a not very wealthy family living in a little house on the winding road that descended to the coast. They'd meet every morning as he accompanied his father to the office. His father, who read something into their meetings, said one day in a voice that was surprisingly not angry, but still authoritative, 'Shall we ask for the hand of this girl?' He blushed bright red, not because he was embarrassed by love, but because his father had said something like this to him for the first time. The rest went like a dream.

There was an elaborate wedding, and for the first time in his life he went without his father on a trip, with his wife. The top storey of the house was allocated to them. Everything was fine despite his father. He loved his wife, but he always wanted to love her even more. When he didn't go to the office, they were always together. His wife did not complain about this. He lived a dream life.

One morning, Semavi Bey saw his father hadn't come down to breakfast. He realised what had happened. An insatiable joy filled him like the sun suddenly coming out on a rainy day. At last it had happened. At last the man he thought he'd never be rid of was no longer. Throughout the week following his father's death, full of religious ceremonies, of the crocodile tears of distant relatives, he had difficulty in disguising his joy. He had gained absolute freedom. There was no longer that cruel figure shaping his life, dividing and ordering his hours, bumping into his days, causing an uproar, interfering with everything: his appearance, his demeanour, his fantasies, or his lust and longing for his wife.

To his wife, when she asked why he wasn't going to work, he'd reply, 'My work is loving you. Every moment I'm away from you gives me pain.' At first she found this natural; she also enjoyed having breakfast with Semavi Bey, lazily reading the paper and going out for a stroll. They spent a few years in this manner. Together they sold the possessions left by his father, together they went shopping or for a stroll. But then this began to irritate his wife.

Semavi Bey wouldn't leave her for a moment. He couldn't stand not touching her, not seeing her face. At night he'd wake up frequently and look to see if she was still beside him. He was overwhelmed by the fear that his wife would leave and not return. Yet his wife, who had grown up without a father and had lost her mother, had nowhere to go even if she wanted to. He didn't leave his wife alone anywhere, not even in the house. She was about to lose her mind.

'One hour!' she begged. 'Leave me for one little hour, please...'

Semavi Bey couldn't understand it. What harm did it do to her? What else was he doing but loving her? His wife was worn out from sobbing, from begging for hours to be able to go somewhere and wander around on her own. She was tired of falling asleep on her bed and finding her husband stroking her hair when she awoke. Occasionally Semavi Bey decided to give his wife some peace, but then he would fall into a panic thinking that she'd leave and never return.

It was one of the last nights of a long, cold winter. The whole city was waiting for spring as though it were waiting to recover from an illness. Semavi Bey had taken his wife out all day; he had tried to entertain her, but he had failed to make her face smile, her face remained darkened by an odd feeling of captivity. They were in the sitting room on the upper floor that overlooked the magnificent view of the Bosphorus. Semavi Bey's wife was punishing him with silence. She was watching the television with vacant eyes and acting as though she didn't hear Semavi Bey's words of love.

Then there was another power cut, a frequent occurrence in those days. His wife got up to light the oil lamp. As she lit it she asked, 'Semavi do you really love me?' This question could have driven Semavi Bey mad. What else did he do? He'd devoted his life and his future to loving his wife. 'Are you never going to let me go?' asked his wife. 'Not even a day, not even an hour?' Semavi Bey found this question ridiculous. After laughing at length he replied, 'Never, not even for a second.'

He could remember that last, long gaze of his wife's. He saw a terrible anger, a desperate rebellion rising from all the cells in her body, growing all of a sudden and settling in her eyes. He saw sparks erupting from his wife's beautiful eyes like a penetrating scream as if the last bit of her strength had been exhausted. The fine-fingered hands that could not be free of this yoke of love went limp and the oil lamp fell on the floor and broke. At first, the flames licked her clothes then climbed quickly, and in a flash enveloped her once beautiful body that seemed withered as though all the blood had drained from it.

The bath attendant finished the newspaper he was reading and stretched himself out lazily. He was hungry. He looked at his watch and decided that it was better to eat now, before the frozen labourers poured in. They'd arrive in twos and threes, chatting and singing songs as they washed and got thoroughly warm. While he was thinking how the best place to get warm in such weather was the bathhouse, the man inside suddenly crossed his mind. He'd not heard a peep out of him for hours. He got up at once and called inside from the cool room, 'Uncle, do you want a scrub?' The only sound he could hear was the dripping water; so he put on his clogs and entered. Then he saw the outstretched body of Semavi Bey stretched out on the marble slab in the centre of the bath. He approached and stared at this fine face twisted with a tragic smile, 'Psst, uncle,' he prodded the shoulder, 'Wake up...'

But Semavi Bey was sleeping so soundly that he clearly had no intention of waking up.

THE SNOW TRAVELLER

Day had broken long ago. The mountains, on whose peaks black clouds settled, sparkled under a cold blue as if signalling the imminent end to the night's pause from the interminable snow of the past few days. A feeble beam of sunlight preparing to warm other parts of the world shone coldly on the railway track that seemed to come from time immemorial and go on to eternity, disrupting and shattering this innocuous, pristine state of nature.

One or two trains that passed during the night had crushed the snow on the railway tracks and turned them into ice. The light reflected from the rails filled the windows of Eşber's desolate, gloomy, two-roomed lodgings, situated a little way from the small town forgotten among the mountains. About a hundred paces from the tin-roofed house, the signal box stood in the shadow of a massive, leaden cloud that would soon cover the whole sky.

Eşber threw a thick log of oak into the cooking stove that rendered this gloomy room completely mournful, and closed the doors of the stove tightly. He placed the large metal jug that he'd filled with ice-cold water on top. The embers inside the stove would burn the log, the water in the jug would heat up, and when Eşber, returned home in the evening, following his snow-covered footprints as if they still existed, he would wash his face and hands with hot water and sit with his back against the wall hanging that depicted drinking deer. He'd take his cigarette packet, his glue and his matches burnt at the end, spend the night with his mind focused on the sounds of the wolves, and the following day he would begin another day just like the previous one.

He'd continue to live in his own troubled, narrow circle, despite the railway which wound along the banks of wild rivers that only showed when the snows melted and passed through deep valleys reaching out to completely different lives. He'd carry on as if there was nothing beyond these steep mountains that enclosed his horizon and the whole world consisted of the belongings and the unrefined, crude feelings that determined his life.

Before putting on his leather jacket, his hat and his gloves, he tore off a leaf of the calendar and read the prayer times, one of the prophet's hadiths on sedition, names to give children yet to be born, the meal for the day, and a short summary of the battle of Uhud, and did not commit a single line to memory. The paper that he held in his hand was not just an ordinary leaf from a calendar, but a document that sustained him by showing how many days were left until spring and reminding him that time was passing. Spring was not a dream. This piece of paper not only told him that to reach spring there were too many days to be counted in haste, but also proved the existence of spring.

Here on the leaf of the calendar that he held in his hand, the presence of a long, hard winter was recorded; a winter too long to pass by getting up and going to bed, cooking lentil soup, collecting burnt matches and making houses out of them. Too long for sitting in the signal box and making telephone calls about delayed trains, waving green-red flags at them that in all their glory spoilt the whiteness stretching to eternity. And too long for exchanging greetings with the engine drivers; asking them for newspapers, ordering salt, sugar and matches; falling asleep at night in front of a constantly snowy TV set; placing a huge bowl in the middle of the room and washing in it; taking his mirror and razor outside for a shave when the rays of the sun suddenly filtered through the snow-laden clouds; brewing tea and drinking it, growing potatoes and cabbage in the garden, feeding chickens, shovelling snow; walking to the small town on market days and buying cheese and village bread; speaking only three or four words a day. These exhausting winters that he'd survived for years made his life resemble a grave illness, to a wavering on the edge of death.

He shut the door that he never felt the need to lock since

there was no one nearby, and went out. He smiled when he saw the tracks of the wolves he heard wandering around his house during the night. The snow that had begun again at daybreak had stopped towards morning; it hadn't yet covered the tracks of the wolves that clawed the door, going berserk with the smell of the three hens that he kept in the spare room of the two-roomed house.

Thank goodness there were wolves in his life. In their eyes he saw savage gleams, while from their healthy, white teeth the blood trickled after their hunt. The struggle between him and them had gradually become a reason for living; it had become a strange game that could only end in blood. He felt for his rifle and remembered the brutality in their bright eyes.

The greatest consolation of this deadly loneliness that ate into his soul like a malignant tumour and turned his face, once young and clear, into a rusty yellow; the thing that transformed life into a game, was this relationship with the wolves. Loneliness gave him unbearable headaches. That's why he took opium when he could find it, and at times like these, like an acrobat walking on a tightrope over a chasm, he'd allow the wolves to get close to him. He enjoyed how they surrounded his house and threatened his life to which, since beginning to spend it in a signal box, he could ascribe no meaning. The hens clucked frantically, frightened by the howling that rent the nights when the madly hungry wolves came down from the mountains; their pitiful clucking drove the wolves even madder, and Eşber took great pleasure in opening his window and firing his rifle at the bright eye of a wolf that had come within claw range. In the mornings of such nights he'd find bloody wolf tracks in the snow. Nature bestowed on him just one colour for the best part of the year: white. This was akin to blindness. Yet the bloody tracks left by a wolf shot in the eye, and the howls that tore and shattered the silence reminded him of his existence. He'd think he didn't exist in this silent whiteness if it weren't for the wolves.

As he walked over to the signal box thinking of the wolves he suddenly spotted the dark blue about to be lost in the snow.

It didn't look anything like the blueness that dominated the sky on spring mornings, or on summer evenings after the sun's redness had disappeared. It could be said perhaps to resemble the blue of matches when they first burst into flame. He couldn't believe his eyes. This blueness he saw in the distance between the forgotten mountains was like the present he'd never received. He went towards the blue that was gently fading under the newly falling snow, took it tenderly in his arms as though taking a budgerigar in the palm of his hand, and walked not to the signal box but towards his home, as the dark blue material flapping against his legs filled him with an indescribable delight.

Then night fell and quickly advanced. Darkness enveloped the surroundings like a mirror reflecting the sad faces of those living in pitiful conditions in small towns and in distant villages among the mountains. It was Fidan whom Eşber had taken in his arms and saved from freezing by bringing her home that morning. Now covered with a woollen blanket, she lay lost in an untroubled and tranquil sleep, watched over and heedless of the passing trains. The howling of the wolves could be heard in the distance. Not that Eşber heard them; for he was waiting for this woman to wake up, this woman with the purest and most beautiful face he'd ever seen.

Fidan suddenly awoke. A mortal fear passed over her face. Then she quickly glanced at the room with a feeling that was a mixture of terror and bewilderment. She saw the wall hanging depicting deer, the steam rising from the lentil soup boiling on the stove, the murmuring TV set, the house of burnt matches on top of it and Eşber who sat at the end of her bed smiling at her.

There was nothing in this smile to evoke a feeling of alarm, or a desire to run away and escape. Quite the contrary, it was innocent, sad and rather bashful. It never occurred to her that this smile would take her from one hell to another; she simply felt a strange relief and began to cry.

Unaware that she'd been pursued by fear for months, Eşber waited for her choking crying to cease, and then whispered,

'Don't be afraid, miss. You have nothing to fear from me.' These words calmed her down; she stretched out her right hand to the wall hanging and touched the deer. Crying, she thought about the morning that had seemed to be the climax of the dark months she'd spent.

She was still afraid when she got on the train that flung her to this strange house among the mountains. But she'd mistaken the music of the train, that began slowly and gradually speeded up, for good news of her own deliverance. Even sharing her compartment with the family with defeated and offended expressions on their faces and baskets and plastic bags stuffed with bundles, had given her an inner peace and a sense of confidence. She would go far away, very far. At the other side of this large country covered with snow, a safe fraternal house would enfold her, and the fear that had hounded her for months would melt away like a piece of ice falling on the stove that heated everything in that house.

She had accumulated a dirty past at a young age, and the fear of death had confronted her at the end of the blind alley she'd entered in order to reach a wonderful, grand life as soon as possible. All night long, half asleep and half awake, she'd thought about what she had suffered; at times she'd awoken in terror, at others she'd visualised her deliverance in between bouts of sleep, and that she'd taken a step towards a safe life. Despite all this broken sleep, however, she'd failed to notice that the large family filling the compartment had got off. So when she found herself utterly alone in the very stuffy compartment in the morning, she was terrified. Defenceless and scared to death.

The men after her were dark and real, in contrast to the infinite whiteness that the train cleaved as it advanced. Their ways were dark. Determined to make her pay a heavy price for attempting to bite off more than she could chew. She'd wandered about the train in the hope of finding another family to shelter with, like the one whose presence had given her security all night, making her feel just a little, safer. But there was no one else on the train except a horde of men twisting their greasy moustaches with their thick stubby fingers and undisguised lust shining in their eyes.

They were many. Realising the safe haven she sought would elude her on this intrepid train courageously travelling to the country's forgotten lands, she'd panicked. She decided she'd go and sit in a compartment that was the most crowded with the men whose lusty stares frightened and overwhelmed her, but whose sheer numbers would protect her.

And that's when it all came to a head.

She didn't know the man whose gun dazzled her with its gleam; she'd never seen him before, but it didn't take her long to realise that he'd been sent by one of those pursuing her, and that he'd been assigned to ambush her. This man, who had closed in on her step by step in a short space of time, was instantly recognisable as one of them: his camel coat thrown over his shoulders, his black eyebrows like a long, thick stroke on his narrow, projecting forehead. This man with his bearing, his style, his unhurried and arrogantly springy walk, and, most important of all, his eyes that seemed to bear no expression, but in which, as he got closer, one could read a lust for brutality – such a man could only be on this train in pursuit of her.

Then two things happened simultaneously: he pulled the trigger and she opened the door to fling herself out. As she rolled in the soft snow, she heard the sound of another shot mingling with the train's melody, and closed her eyes in peace. Even if she died it no longer mattered. She hadn't fallen into 'their' hands. If she *had* died at that moment, it would have been a very quiet and peaceful departure towards death.

Now, in this strange room, where she felt her stiff body relaxed utterly and jelly-like, she was crying with relief; unable to believe she'd returned from the brink of death. She could not stop her tears as she ate the bowl of soup Eşber offered.

'Thank you,' she said. 'You saved my life.'

Eşber didn't answer. He gazed with a gentle, shy smile that contrasted with the savageness surrounding this house of breeze blocks and stone, wattle and daub. In his world, life was something that was frequently saved. He saved his own life yet again in every game with the wolves. That's why it wasn't something worth thanking. Fidan ate her soup, wiped her eyes and looked at the heart-warming white teeth of this sallow-faced man who'd saved her life. She was now sure that she was safe. Eşber brewed some tea, sat cross-legged on the same chair, and gazed at her face with an expression that asked her what she was doing by the railway line. The small town was quite some distance, nowhere near the railway and, even if it had been, trains wouldn't stop at this tiny little town that lived quietly among the mountains. Whatever had made the woman in the blue coat set off on a path that led to his gloomy, mournful house?

Fidan felt that she had to speak, to tell him something, and so she made up a little story: she was a lawyer, and the brothers of a man she'd had thrown into prison were after her, and just as they were about to kill her, she'd thrown herself off the train.

Eşber believed this at once. The ever snowy TV set whose sound he had to content himself with had taught him there was a large and complicated world outside. Out there, there were crowds of people. A merciless battle raged, like his war with the wolves. The traces of fear on the face of the slim, beautiful woman who said her name was Fidan were proof of this too. He asked a heap of questions about the world beyond the mountains. He was trying to understand a different kind of savagery. Fidan answered in a soft voice that caressed his spirit, and she told him a lot of things about crowded cities, reinforcing her dark story. The good quality cigarettes in her bag ran out that night; she smoked Eşber's cheaper cigarettes and quickly got used to them.

Late in the night she heard the sound of the wolves. The addicts of this deadly game arrived one by one and surrounded the house, while the hens clucked in fear. Eşber kept his composure as the wolves howled. He told her that there was nothing to be frightened of; he eschewed the game that the wolves longed for. Then he left Fidan in the warm, cosy room with the roaring stove, rolled out a bed for himself and went to sleep in the room where the hens were.

Eşber believed that night he'd been blessed with a divine gift, and slept in peace. As for Fidan; she contemplated all night long. She had informed on the men pursuing her. She could stay in this strange house for a long time, until they were caught, and they all believed that she was dead; she could wipe out traces of her own life, and *then* she could think about what she needed to do when she returned to her own city. She lay, pressing her hand against the wall hanging of deer and staring at the darkness. She was petrified with the terror of the days of constantly running away, and the possibility of coming face to face with death at any moment. Just then, the terrifying sounds of the wolves were like an innocent song compared with the feeling of brutality she had in the city.

She awoke in the morning to see Eşber filling up the stove. The sallow-faced man had been up a long time, had made tea and was waiting for his guest to wake up, keeping his own movements as quiet as possible. They breakfasted on village bread and village cheese. Then Eşber pointed out the signal box to her from the window. That's where he would be. There was nothing to be frightened of. He wanted her to tell him if there was anything she wanted. He could order it from the engine drivers.

Fidan passed the day in high spirits. For the first time in a long period she experienced peace. She slept all day on the couch and whenever she woke up she couldn't believe she was alive.

On the following days it kept snowing and stopping. The times that it snowed were more than the times that it stopped. Sometimes it turned Eşber into a snowman before he'd even taken two paces towards the two square-metered signal box to wave a flag at the passing trains, and sometimes it mixed with the sunrays, and made the mountaintops look as if they had been sprinkled with gold dust. Fidan never left the house; she threw wood on the stove that Eşber filled to the brim and lit every morning, and staring at the wall hanging of deer, she thought about herself and her future. Even if she was bored just sitting there, she made herself believe that this hiding was essential in order for her to survive. She lit and blew out Eşber's matches one by one as she convinced herself of this.

The long conversations they held every evening had gradually driven the yellow hue from Eşber's face. A curious joy filled him and made him forget the wolves. He felt an unfamiliar attachment to life. He no longer needed the wolves in order to exist. A woman talking, smiling, eating every evening had filled his house, life and mind. He'd begun to take an interest in his wages. Now he talked more with the engine drivers of the trains that slowed down to a crawl as they approached the signal box, asking them to bring newspapers, books, good quality tea and cigarettes. He had changed. He always used to drag his feet home as if heading to a fatal loneliness; now he went home overflowing with the desire to live. In his hut, while waiting for a train that was to change points, he'd stare at the house seen from the window and he'd remember a woman was sitting there, and this feeling would exhilarate him.

He'd think about Fidan's hair that scattered sunlight, the dimple that appeared in only one cheek when she smiled, and her hands as white as snow. He would feel an emptiness in his breast, an emptiness that he thought would fill only if he pressed her sweet-smelling hair to it. This emptiness within him was the motivation that drove him to the irrepressible joy that the even drivers noticed, and it was the reason for him feeling a deep ache from the knowledge that he could not hug her warm blonde head.

At times, the knowledge that a woman was living in his house unbeknownst to everyone drove him to an incomprehensible exuberance. He got excited as though this fact was a terrific secret that interested the whole world, and not to shout this woman's existence to the mountains and not to tell anyone this incredible thing was like a heavy weight which crushed him. Sometimes he had the impression that the merry voice of a woman filling his nights and the white, slim fingers that burnt his skin like fire when they touched it by accident, were not real, that all this was a fabrication of his mind as it slowly dyed in the face of the blinding whiteness. He'd run to the house from the hut to test this reality time and again, and when he arrived breathless, he'd be confronted with Fidan's eyes asking why he had come; then he'd just stand at the door, bewildered and without an answer, like a sleepwalker who had awoken from a deep sleep.

In the course of a single day, he would pass through a whole range of mental states. Now he no longer waited for spring, although it was just around the corner. It seemed that winter spring had come to his house in an unexpected form, in any case. He had no idea how to make this unexpected spring happy; too shy to ask her what she wanted, he followed her every move all night long, hoping to understand what she desired.

This heart that was used to being silent, trapped as if shut in a box, opened up and spoke without stopping. Eşber's speech did not follow a sequence, but jumped from one subject to another. He passed from the daughter of his sister, living in a distant, but warm small town, who could not say her r's, to the noise made by the snow as it melted, and while talking about the habits of the engine drivers, the low wages in line with village expectations, or the deliciousness of the ewe's cheese of a nearby village, he'd suddenly jump to the flocks of birds descending on the mountains, the sounds dispersing the silence and the spirit of the mountains. This leaping about and these weird descriptions scared Fidan.

That wasn't all that scared her. She had begun to see love in Eşber's eyes. She saw that while she spoke he didn't listen to her, but was engrossed in her eyes, her hands and her body; that he'd grown strange; that whenever she swallowed a bite it was as if he was swallowing a bite, and whenever she took a drag it was as if Eşber was smoking a cigarette. The fear she'd forgotten took on a different aspect and slowly seeped inside her.

One night she asked the whereabouts of the small town. Eşber pointed with his hand in a vague direction and said, 'Behind those mountains...' the tone of his voice tinged with the morbid superiority of having described an unattainable peak. The expression dominating his face was so strange and scary that

Fidan never repeated this question she'd asked innocently, and to which she received no answer; so she never learnt behind which mountain the small town lay.

Many long nights and days went by with more sound and words than this dismal house had ever heard.

Fidan decided it was now time to go. Never mind those on her tail: it was enough of this interminable whiteness, of the unremitting snow that made her believe it would swallow the house and the wolves that wandered around every night and in whose sounds she had begun to sense a call for blood, Eşber's obsession was increasingly becoming more morbid, and the days that passed all seemed exactly the same and had begun to frighten her almost as much as the sinister men following her. She sensed Eşber would not be content with gazing at her passionately, but want her to share his life. This was living another life, wearing a dress not her own. That last night all she could think about was this. And because she didn't sleep, she noticed how much wilder the sounds of the wolves were than she'd previously thought.

The next morning, Eşber came into the room to brew the tea, and went white as a sheet upon seeing Fidan holding the bag that was on her shoulder when she threw herself from the train and wearing the blue coat that had filled him with an indescribable joy as it flapped against his knees while he was carrying her.

'What's the matter?' he asked, 'Why have you got dressed?'

'I should go now,' said Fidan, trying to sweeten her voice as much as possible,

'I'm so grateful to you for everything. But I've stayed long enough. My parents will be looking for me. They must be worried about me. Could you put me on the train?'

'No,' said Eşber. 'No, it's just not possible, you can't go.'

'Why not?'

Eşber reached out, pulled Fidan's bag and hurled it onto the couch.

'You came to me...' he said, staring as if he couldn't believe what was happening.

He really couldn't believe it. Fidan was a spring sent to him, something that belonged to him, appearing in front of him like a miracle sent to eliminate his pathetic loneliness, to fill his silent hours, his empty days. It wasn't possible for him to endure her going just like that, to put her on the train with his own hands.

'Aren't you comfortable here?' he asked, his face bewildered, his voice that was as mild as could be,

The expression on his face was akin to that of a well-intentioned master addressing his slave, a master who reserves all rights of disposal: sweet and innocent, but equally merciless.

Fidan realised at that moment that this was the beginning of a tremendous battle between them, one that would only end with death. She went weak at the knees, her body, that had stood erect while those terrible men pursued her, forever resisting and rushing from house to house, street to street, spending each night under a different roof and enduring this relentless race for days dissolved in an instant when confronted with this mild, calm question, and collapsed to the ground.

The first thing she did was to shut up. She sensed the futility of trying to persuade this man, whose mind the mountains and snow had virtually sucked up and then left to his own devices, and so she wouldn't say anything. She was frightened that a word sticking in his mind like a needle could drive this man, this dervish of a strange world, crazy. She'd fallen into his hands; Eşber was lord of this eternal whiteness. That night, the following night and the nights after, she remained silent. Eşber talked. This man, who had long since finished talking about himself, and whose face had gradually regained its original sallowness since the day Fidan announced she wanted to leave, related one by one whatever remained in his mind from the calendar leaves, whatever the railway employees from large crowded cities told him, and whatever he'd heard on the television he listened to, and which opened his dreams to distant places. But whatever he did, he couldn't make Fidan laugh, or bring back the dimple on her cheek that he so wanted to touch or even kiss, and this ate his heart out.

One day, Fidan came out of the house and just stood under the snow. It was as though she had fallen into a white labyrinth with no signs on it. Where was east? In which direction was west and how could one get to the town? She could not find the answers to these questions and realised to what extent she was a real prisoner. As she surrendered her whole self to nature to find a way out, perhaps by feel or by smell, her nose in the air, Eşber watched her through the signal box window steamed up by his breath, a sickly smile heightening the pitiful expression on his face. From now on, the point of his life was to protect this spring that had come to him unseasonably, and hang onto it to eternity. He never took his eyes off the door of the house; if Fidan came out, he suddenly appeared beside her; he ordered presents and fresh fruit for her and, even though he could get nothing in return, he was content with things continuing in this manner.

Fidan had realised daytime trains would be of no use; it was a night-time train that attracted her attention. This unassuming train would come quietly as midnight approached, its growls softly seeping into the house, and the lights of the passenger carriages were reflected as fast-moving images in the windows covered by the night. Because that was the only night-time train, Eşber would make way for it in the evening and then come home. The train climbed up a gentle slope to the snow-covered plain and slowed down to a crawl as it passed Eşber's house. Fidan felt her deliverance lay with this train, but she just couldn't find the way to board it and leave.

It was a particularly harsh winter night, despite spring being just around the corner. The cooking stove was making short work of the logs of wood and the windows were covered with a thin sheet of ice. A silence had fallen on Eşber. He was peeling oranges he'd ordered from the engine drivers in thin strips, as if threatening Fidan for her silence. He had the air of a master coming to the end of his tether. His state of mind had begun to scare Fidan.

She heard the howling of the wolves as she waited for the sound of the train that came silently, and passing through the mountains went on to crowded, brightly lit towns where safety lay. They were descending from the mountains again. Fidan thought for a moment that they were free. They could run for hours after a train if they wanted, or die if they wanted. She sighed. Eşber, on the other hand, was beginning to chafe at this never-ending silence. When he heard the howling of the wolves he got up and opened the window, startling Fidan. The room felt like it was filled with air full of broken pieces of ice. Fidan shivered from the cold and the savage howling. Eşber took his rifle down from the wall, the one he took with him every day when he went to the signal box, and waited for the wolves to surround the house, to approach. The hens had begun to cluck frantically again, terrified of the imminent danger. Eşber was leaning out of the window and shouting at the wolves, attracting their attention and preparing for the game that he hadn't played since Fidan's arrival, and that he very much missed. The wolves gathered by the window. Their sound was unnerving. Fidan was trembling from head to foot. She was scared to death and didn't know what to do. Eşber raised his rifle and took aim at the eye of a wolf, but just as he was about to fire Fidan cried, 'Don't' and threw herself at him. The rifle went off and a very thin spark trailed skywards. The wolves scattered.

This word that came from Fidan's mouth for the first time in days stunned Eşber. He felt pain as if he'd hurt her, threw down the rifle and stared at her, distraught. It threw him into an odd state that he could not comprehend. He sank to the ground and began to stare at Fidan without taking his eyes off her. He seemed to be waiting for an order from her. He looked weird and pathetic.

Fidan shut her eyes and two images appeared in her mind. In one were the wolves: eyes gleaming like steel, with powerful jaws and sharp claws, and howls that sent shudders down her spine, and Eşber stood in the other. This was such a daunting picture; he was staring at her from the signal box window, the tick in his right cheekbone making his sickly smile even more terrifying.

She heard the sound of the train climbing the slope between the subsiding howls of the wolves. She thought about the passengers in those compartments, wrapping their foul-smelling cheese in their thin flat bread and eating it; their vacant eyes fixed on a distant point, smoking cigarettes slowly and seeing their own sad faces in the windows. When it was morning they'd be getting off in a bright, crowded city, and, shouldering their loads, they'd scatter into the city's mud-covered arteries and mingle with the crowds to take their places on the stages that life had prepared for them. Even if dark-faced men existed there in that life, a hope of escape could always be found. This was to walk freely, even towards the danger of death that awaited her. All this crossed her mind in a very short space of time and she opened her eyes and looked at Eşber. Eşber was sitting as though mesmerised.

Sensing that this mesmerised moment was not going to last long, she suddenly jumped up. She had on a thin jumper and only socks on her feet. With tremendous courage and strength she opened the door and threw herself outside. It was snowing, snow that soon would turn to a blizzard, as the train that would take her to life advanced reluctantly. She began to run through the snow, sinking every step of the way. She heard the sounds of the wolves, which strangely didn't frighten her. As if the wolf whose eye she'd saved just now would protect her from all danger.

She saw the train passing in front of the house and was running to reach this miraculous means of transportation that scattered sparks from its wheels, to this iron heap emitting growls, but the snow in which she sank to her knees was holding her back. She heard Eşber's voice echoing in the darkness of the night. Not a voice but a blood-curdling wail. He was saying, 'Don't go!' He was calling her.

She had got to the door of the train, and managed to reach up and open it, but she just could not get on. She could only run alongside the moving carriages. She felt Eşber was getting very close, could almost feel his breath, but didn't dare look behind her. Then she felt a hand grab her jumper and drag her down as if dragging her to death. She knew she'd die if she didn't board the train. Despite Eşber's powerful hands still tugging at her jumper, she managed to leap on board, and grab the steel handle of the train door with all the strength in her frozen hands. Snow was filling her eyes, and the icy wind created by the train was overpowering her.

Fidan heard the wolves, their howls now growing frenzied. And then the force pulling her was gone. When she looked back, she saw the wolves surrounding Eşber.

But she had no desire to contemplate who would win this game that she'd witnessed for the first time.

MIKAIL'S HEART STOPPED

Mikail's heart just stopped. His heart stopped suddenly at the end of a cold, weary night of reckoning while trying to hide, not his crying, but his crying from the pain of defeat. It stopped in the house where brackish water seeped through the walls and where he lived in tragic taciturnity and poverty with his two small children, whose missing teeth remained as such from lack of care, and his wife, from whose lips poured anguished curses.

I know precisely the moment his heart stopped. For, at the exact moment when Mikail's heart stopped I awoke in fright from a sweaty and almost unconscious sleep, stabbed in the heart not by his resentful knife, dulled from always being held in his palm, but by his resentful eyes. I knew this from learning the time of death that spread immediately through the weary neighbourhood of the town that lived like a diseased lung taking groaning, deep breaths. I looked at Semiramis sleeping beside me exhaling hot breaths redolent of alcohol, unaware of this deep wound I'd received.

'Mikail's heart has stopped,' I whispered. Then I repeated this sinister sentence, unwilling to even believe it myself: 'Mikail's heart has stopped!' Semiramis didn't hear; she drew up her bare legs to her flabby stomach. I huddled up in her wide, comfortable bed and became insignificant. I couldn't go back to sleep again.

From that day on I lost sleep. You could say I lost peace of mind. I wanted to sleep, to roll in sleep's deep, delicious nothingness and at least forget for one night that mental anguish. But no. The moments I slept were so brief that they were only enough for me to forget Mikail's old-fashioned moustache extending like a spindly lament, dividing his lifeless face grown rapidly old in pursuit of a deadly obsession. I could not banish his doleful eyes from my mind, those eyes that had taken on the helplessness of a sacrificial animal, and that had long ago ceased being angry with me.

Even though I'd succeeded in forgetting Mikail for brief moments, I just couldn't escape from his spirit which seemed to be virtually living with me. In every mirror I always saw Mikail's touching face. I told this pale ghost that my only crime was to be caught up in a strange eddy, accidentally finding myself in the most seething part of a life to which I was in fact a stranger. But still I tossed and turned in my bed in anguish, asking myself why I couldn't have an uninterrupted, tranquil sleep.

I answered at once: *Because I'm guilty. I stole something. For me it was something worthless and even vulgar. But I stole it.*

First I left Semiramis to be rid of this pain no one knew about, but that made my heart seep blood. As I packed my suitcase (my constant companion through years of roaming in search of a peaceful, quiet place under a bed) the unkempt heads of women stretching out from wretched apartments on the dreary street talked in most heart-wrenching words about Mikail's house a few streets away where his sallow-faced, poor relatives went in and out, and his thin wife held her two children by the hand during the lonely and exceedingly simple funeral, crying non-stop, 'What am I going to do now?' They said this wretched death was Mikail's destiny as their eyes sought Semiramis at the window. As I packed slowly, a deep ache in my heart, Semiramis kept her silence, knowing that asking me to stay would be no use. Even if we had not spoken about it, she was aware of the strange battle between us.

Semiramis is very much to blame for this silent hostility. You could even say that it was her devilish smile, that first night I saw Mikail, that had provoked me to take sides in this pathetic quarrel. But this could also be an excuse I found for myself. It is also possible that Semiramis had done what was right by her own judgement. I might have been the only one in the wrong. If I'd known the night I first saw Mikail, as I looked arrogantly down at him in his ridiculous outfit and with his old-fashioned moustache, that one day he would hurt me in this way, I would never have stayed in this world of dark people. Their exaggerated cheerfulness was woven with genuine sorrows, to which I knew full well I didn't belong, but I just couldn't leave because I so relished the state of pretentious foreignness. I should have left at one of the times when, though it was just the right time to go, I was not able to because I was carried away in the pleasure of laziness.

I first saw Mikail on a terrifically hot summer's night, when not a leaf moved and all the windows of the city were wide open.

This bizarre district was groaning with hear, yet Semiramis was loyally bound to it because it had welcomed her to its festering bosom in her times of poverty when she had lived through thousands of heartaches and humiliation. The smell of blood that flowed from the broken noses of women beaten every night and the echo of the normally accepted violence of strong against weak accepted was absent for once. It was as though a break had been taken from the brutal and sinful nightlife of the district. The street dogs were silent and the street urchins had stretched out full length on the stones warmed up during the day. Even the flies were not flying.

We had stretched out on the sofa in the sitting room whose high ceilings gave at least a little feeling of airiness, and were drinking beer with vodka. I'd laid my head on Semiramis's ample bosom that had now gone really soft. She messed my hair with fingers adorned with tasteless, but expensive rings as she told me why she had changed her name from Semra into Semiramis. And as I listened to her I was thinking that we were by no means, and would never be, made of the same stuff. This thought really cheered me. I felt like a daring criminal wandering around boldly in places that didn't belong to me.

Semiramis' old photographs and the self-confidence that she possessed even now that she was past her prime, attested to the fact that she was once very beautiful. But she had become a drunk, as was deemed necessary for a music hall partner. She confidently told me how she succeeded in having her say in her own world because she was cleverer than the women who could only exist in this world of nights as long as their bodies were fresh. And all the time she was planning to hold me in her hand by offering lust, femininity and an endless wallowing in irresponsible nothingness: a place well beyond the understanding of those who pay their bills on time, live in good, strong houses, and consider themselves very proper.

Many men had entered her life. Although she had loved none, she'd succeeded in getting something useful from each one. Good advice from some, as much money as she could comfortably spend from others, a few items of jewellery that they were willing to sacrifice to prolong a sickly obsession a little longer from yet others, and a few sweet memories from others still. From some, she even learnt something. An elderly, well educated man, ugly and grumpy but sweet-smelling, whose mistress she was when she'd freshly set out in pursuit of the splendour that she now inhabited and enjoyed, said precisely this to her: 'The Semiramises wreck the clumsy, happy-looking homes that the Semras strived to make.'

Whether he was a lunatic who'd made her learn this sentence by heart out of a wish to engrave such witticisms in the heads of his mistresses, or whether it was Semiramis's own slight revulsion to Semras' provincial docility that made her want to learn it by heart, I don't know. But just as Semiramis, the deliberate *femme fatale*, uttered this sentence, the bell rang at length with pathetic insistence. That devilish smile, rarely to be found on the face of Semras better suited to compassion, appeared briefly on Semiramis's face. I stared at her wondering why she wouldn't open the door. 'That's Mikail,' she said, 'He'll keep ringing and then go away.'

A man who imploringly rang the bell of a door that didn't open, and then went away. Mikail. Semiramis got up lazily and defying the heat, sauntered to the bathroom in fluid movements of her still attractive body clad in the black underwear that drove the men she knew to a vulgar pleasure. I sensed she took great delight in not opening the door to Mikail. I heard her step into the shower. The sound of the water comforted my spirit. Remembering her brief, devilish smile, I wanted to see Mikail; the man who had to go because the door that at one time probably opened wide, opened no longer.

This door had been opened to me although I'd not promised anything, and I could keep it open for as long as I wanted. Not that his mattered to me in the slightest. Semiramis was a clever, but common woman. An old coquette, whom I could leave whenever I wanted and, even if she did cry after me, had been through the mill enough to forget me quickly. My reason for not going was not that Semiramis surrendered to me with all her being, but because of my own laziness to look for a new place, an abode, a different world. I was one of the lost children. I'd surrendered myself to the sickly feelings of defeat and my sense of being lost without a future.

Pride may be the last thing one would feel in this deep void he believes has swallowed his soul. All the same, I just couldn't stop myself. I went to the window to see Mikail, or rather, to flaunt myself. He'd already come down the steps that he'd ascended just now in hopeful and confident steps. His head was bent and he was probably upset as he turned into the narrow street, his chest hardened with the bitterness it harboured. Did he lift his head and look at the window just as he was going because he thought that another man lived in this house that he could no longer enter, and he wanted to see the face that had taken his place? I don't know. Our eyes met in the light of the street lamp.

I saw his black eyes. Despite the tense, harsh expression on his face, to me they looked very sad. He wore a light-weight black jacket and he had pulled the collar of his white shirt over the top. He looked at me for a few seconds, touched his moustache and in a few hasty paces, got into his Anadol estate he'd parked in front of the door. I didn't know it at the time, but it was full to the brim with kitchenware. It was quite obvious he preferred to pretend not to see me. I was just looking without a single feeling of rivalry and passion, just out of a funny carefree drunkenness, to which I had abandoned myself-. My earlier pride had also gone. I was no different from a bored old woman, spying on the shadows of the neighbours' windows that filtered light. Yet I was to understand at our second meeting that Mikail saw me as a rival.

There was a pathetic urgency in his manner, a resentment that he tried ineptly to conceal. He was ashamed as though the whole street knew that the door on which he had knocked hadn't opened. It was as though, by pretending not to see me, he was acting nobly in his own way and giving Semiramis and me another chance. That's why he wanted to leave the street as quickly as possible. He got into his car wishing to immediately forget the short eye contact between us. He turned the key, but the tired Anadol that had roamed the streets all day long just wouldn't start. I felt the palms of his hands sweating and his deep humiliation because the car, in spite of his turning the key, time and again and making it tweet like a wounded bird, still refused to start.

Unable to start the car, he was forced to get out. Dripping with sweat, and with one hand on the steering wheel, he began to push the Anadol that could hardly move because of its load. The dispirited Anadol, happy with the front of the door where it was parked, and looking as if it would happily rest in eternal peace, eventually began to slide down the slope. Mikail ran in funny steps and got in. The Anadol growled a little with the intention of starting as it was about to disappear. The thundering noise of the old engine reverberated in the street and gradually moved out of sight. The street returned to the cloying silence of a little while before. I went inside. Remembering Mikail's state and laughing, I lay back on Semiramis's enormous bed. I must have gone to sleep...

Now when I think about it, after starting his wreck of an Anadol and reaching the main road, Mikail might have stopped the car, put his head on the vinyl-covered steering wheel and cried in frustration.

In this world of strange street credibility, where life was lived through primitive feelings and weird ceremonies, where even a little slip of the foot could flatten one's honour in a trice, the situation into which Mikail had fallen was a heavy blow. If the Anadol, worn out from the bustle of life, had started at the first turn of the key, and Mikail been able to leave the street with a swanky start, perhaps this silent struggle between us would never have begun.

It was not the rivalry of love that destroyed him, but the little mishaps that befell him.

I slept and forgot all about him. I cast him completely out of my mind. And so when we met again a few days later in the street where Semiramis lived, I had difficulty in recognising him. Semiramis had got work in a coastal town and gone on tour with a few girls who worked in a music hall. I imagine she was expecting *not* to find me on her return. She had regarded this tour as a test of love and, because she didn't want me to leave her, she'd filled the fridge with a great variety of food. That night we never slept at all, just drank non-stop. Towards morning she cried at length because one day I would leave her for sure. I made no attempt to comfort her. She was exhausted from drinking and lack of sleep. As soon as she got on the coach she passed out. Overflowing with an uncalled for feeling of freedom, I went to the parts of the city I'd not visited for a long time, dozing in tea gardens with my head resting on the tables. I stared at myself in still waters. I looked for some small joy inside myself. A new path. It was so hot I couldn't find one.

Even though it was just the right time to go, I was seduced by the idea of going to bed yawning lazily in a room that was cool when the windows were wide open. Or perhaps my motive was sheer laziness, and this delicious laziness that I profoundly felt towards life was what made me drag my feet again towards Semiramis's house. In any case, it was impossible to make even the simplest plan, let alone take a crucial decision, while groaning under the sticky, July heat.

As I walked in pensive steps I got distracted by the heads of women leaning out their windows, cracking black sunflower seeds and spitting the husks onto the street. From the opposite direction came the tired old Anadol, running with a groan, its loud noise filling the street. After Mikail parked his car in front of the door to the block of flats, got out and struck a smart pose, I recognised him by the moustache that had attracted my attention that first night I saw him. It was obvious that for this meeting he'd had the broken Anadol repaired, had dressed with care and even rehearsed the show that was to be exhibited to the neighbourhood. He'd coloured his hair and deliberately left a few strands of grey hair on the temples.

All of a sudden he spotted me. For a moment, he got very nervous, very upset. Then he pulled himself together. We were eye to eye. He put his hand to his pocket to take out his flick knife. But he couldn't find his pocket. When I saw his white socks that the turn-ups of his trousers – shrunk from being washed so many times – couldn't conceal and how this ruined his flashy stance, I couldn't help but laugh. I walked towards the apartment without changing my step. At last he found his pocket, took out his flick knife and began to open and close it. There was a very short distance between us.

The knife that Mikail wanted to see in my heart failed to impress me in the slightest. It was as though my soul had voided. The gleam of this sharp steel had as little meaning for me as the tail of a cat crossing the street in a rush. In fact, I myself walked with a wish to add meaning to that knife and to feel it in my heart. I didn't care about being one of the lost children. This feeling was so strong that even if that knife stuck in my heart I felt unreal enough to be able to wander around with it. And so I walked towards the knife. Not as an act against Mikail nor to have my name remembered in the world of heroism. The courage he derived from the knife wasn't enough for him and I saw how his hands were shaking.

With only a few steps between me and the knife, a woman whose large, heavy earrings had slit her earlobes came out of the opposite block, dragging a runny-nosed girl who clutched her skirt. She approached Mikail, coming right between us and asked, 'Have you got a set of coffee pots?'

A little mishap that Mikail had just not reckoned on ruined the whole scene. A crowd of women surrounded the Anadol estate full of kitchenware for sale. Dozens of calloused, reddened, swollen women's hands opened the boot of the car that was slightly ajar, and began to rummage through it.

All of a sudden he'd been dragged away from the film in which he starred, and was besieged by women asking the prices of the frying pans, pressure cookers and ladles they had grabbed, ready to bargain hard. It was impossible for him to disrupt this crowd of women driven wild by that obsession called shopping and continue the film. While he was trying to save his goods from the hands of the women, I entered the block, fully enjoying this ludicrous situation. I went upstairs and looked from the window.

He knew I was watching him. That's why he never bothered to look like a simple salesman, sweet talking to sell his goods in order to earn a few pennies. He was so angry and so hurt that he roughly gathered all his goods and filled his car. Then he got into it, shaking with rage. Unable to understand the reason for this behaviour from a man from whom they'd been buying goods for a long time, the women dispersed to their homes, shouting abuse and even swearing at him.

The Anadol, that on our previous encounter had spited him by not starting, started this time by emitting appalling noises. He took no notice of the clanking of the boot door that was up in the air because he hadn't shut it. As he shot through the street the children scattered in all directions; he scraped an electricity pole and hit a dustbin. When he emerged onto the main road, the dustbin he'd hit rolled, clanging down the street like a spectator rolling about laughing at the state into which he had fallen.

After this incident I didn't see Mikail for a long time. We never met. But some time later I felt that he was following me. He was as silent as a professional killer wanting to perform a clean job. He never showed himself. But I always knew he was after me and felt his breath on the back of my neck. I enjoyed this so much that some nights I'd suddenly turn back along the streets I walked. Sometimes I met with the sound of feet running rapidly away so as not to be caught. Sometimes a deep silence. The nights that he didn't follow me became boring. I could have been lost in a delightful game woven with illusions and I was curious about the conclusion.

In the beginning, he wanted to frighten me away. Then later, he wanted to kill me. All he really wanted was to regain Semiramis who had now closed her doors to him in spite of me. He thought I was the sole reason the door wouldn't open despite his ringing the bell time and again. This was really funny, to be honest. And besides, both in Mikail's state, and in the strange bond between us, there was a sad, weird thing like a fit of crying after laughing too much. To me, Semiramis was nothing; to him, she was everything. To Semiramis, Mikail was nothing and I was everything.

I began to go to the music hall every evening, just for the pleasure of having him follow me. This made Semiramis very happy. She mistook it for some kind of commitment. And in fact it was. But not to Semiramis. To my executioner.

I am now through with the song of darkness and reside in a distant, peaceful, humdrum town where I show a reluctant effort to join the ranks of proper people. Yet I miss not Semiramis, but the music hall that breathed with sorrowful breaths even though it is common, even though it is crude, faithless and wretched. That place was a badly sung song of darkness. Just like the flaws in the voices of singers, the plaintive place where life's heavy blows leave deep scars on faces, the place which has taken refuge in the pretence of bright lights...

It was in the music hall one night that I came to realise that Mikail had given up scaring me and decided to kill me. Semiramis had, with one eye on me, sat down at the table of a customer whose mistress she had probably once been. I was quietly drinking with my back to the stage at the bar, and so was as much of a stranger to the interior as me

I was staring in the cheap mirror at my expressionless face of indeterminate age. I felt as though I'd lived a thousand years, and that feeling aroused a deep sadness. I asked myself why I was such a stranger to my own life. I was going to ask myself much more, but I snapped out of myself when I heard Mikail's name in the conversation between the barman and the waiter nearby. I didn't know whether they knew he had at one time been Semiramis's lover. It never interested me in the slightest how much those in the music hall knew about this skein of strange entanglements that linked the three of us together. In any case, no one but Mikail had interested me.

The barman and waiter spoke on, unaware I was listening. Mikail had sold his Anadol estate to buy a weapon. But the man who'd taken the money and said he'd get him a Parabellum had disappeared. At that moment I remembered that I hadn't heard the sound of the tired Anadol starting with mournful screams for a long time. The barman laughed at this sad deception. 'Who was he going to shoot with that weapon?' he asked. The waiter said, 'Who knows. Perhaps he is going to shoot himself...'

I didn't meet Mikail at all until the end of the summer. He was no longer following me as frequently as he used to. Perhaps he'd gone after the man who went off with his money promising to bring him a weapon. Even so, I felt he might be following me, and some nights while walking in the streets that stretched out pitch dark, when I occasionally turned and looked behind me, I'd catch sight of a shadow sheltering in the entrances to apartments, a shadow that had gradually grown weaker and thinner.

Then summer came to an end. I thought he'd got tired of following me.

It was an October evening. There were signs of an early winter in the air. A filthy drizzle smothered this city, tired existing in an even worse gloom. Semiramis had gone again on one of those shitty tours. I wandered about the streets watching the death of this unfortunate city. I looked at the clouds that sank on it like a dirge. I climbed high hills to see if I could spot a vein through which perhaps clean blood still flowed, in the hope that it would excite me and spur me to go somewhere new. Nothing excited me. Not even the rain that wet my face and my hair and made me cold. The notion of going away for a new beginning seemed so difficult; impossible even. I returned to Semiramis's house knowing I was fast growing old there.

Darkness had yet to fall when I entered the street. The rain that had fallen intermittently, forming futile puddles in the street, had ceased. The air was still heavy. The street's futureless and hopeless children were playing ball.

I found Mikail at the entrance to Semiramis's block of flats. He'd turned up the collar of his threadbare jacket and crouched on the paved area in front of the door. He'd leant his head against the wall and, tired of waiting for me for hours, he'd fallen asleep. I approached him and stood looking. His beard had grown. There was not a trace of his old self. He was snoring lightly. I wanted him to wake up and see me and plunge his resentful knife right into my heart. But he didn't look like he'd wake up. I leant over and tapped his shoulder. I wanted to say, 'Wake up. Wake up and save me from this never-ending nothingness with the knife you are going to stab into my chest!' He didn't wake up.

Just then a ball one of the children kicked smashed into his face. He woke up suddenly, leapt up without seeing me and walked towards the children, swearing. He caught the ball and slashed it with the knife he'd imagined in my heart. That's when our eyes locked. Ball and knife fell from his hands.

The truth of the matter is that he was unlucky enough to drive someone to suicide.

From that day onward he definitely stopped following me. We still met from time to time. Whenever he saw me he would quickly turn his back and walk away with hasty steps. He had become very thin, as though this defeat had finished him off. He didn't pass the streets I did and never visited the places where I might be. One day, we met in a neighbourhood market. He'd arranged a few dozen Paşabahçe glasses on a small stand. To attract the attention of the passers-by he was juggling three glasses in the air and calling out to the women who looked at him as they passed. When he spotted me, he failed to catch the glasses.

I heard his circumstances deteriorated even more, and he aged a lot after our encounter. Presumably he had thought at length about it all, and deciding that luck was with me, had given up. Now, because he didn't follow me, I left off going to the music hall. I killed time thinking about life, about people and about Mikail, and things that were not at all funny, and I drank. The absence of the man whom I'd destroyed by stealing his greatest love and frittering away the love that I stole had shaken me badly. I used to laugh when I thought about him. Until I no longer could. I realised this was akin to cutting my wrists in hot water. While I was cutting my wrists I felt no pain, but now my spirit was smarting.

I was drinking so much that one night I realised I'd drunk the house dry. It was very late and there wasn't anything open. I had no choice but set out for the music hall. It was a snowy night and the streets were covered with ice. I wandered along the very back alleys where the dirtiest blood of the city was shed. I walked among the street urchins warming their dirty hands over fires they lit in tin barrels; the homeless preparing to lie down on the cardboard that they spread out in sheltered corners; the juvenile glue sniffers cuddling thin street cats; transvestites in the middle of a fight or recovering from one; street dogs howling from cold and hunger, all fear of humans long since forgotten. And while I walked through all this, I noticed I was following a black, sagging overcoat.

He'd sat down in the most deserted corner of a bar, and was drinking beer, his head bent forward. Silently I came and sat beside him. He didn't move at all, nor did he lift his head to look. Just as I was thinking he hadn't recognised me, he said in a shaky voice, his eyes fixed on his beer glass, 'I used to have a glass and china shop. I used to sell glassware. She wanted lots of things; I used to buy them. Then you came along. Now I have nothing...'

He drained the glass and wiped his mouth with the back of his shaking hand. In a voice that was not indignant, not hostile, not angry but harrowing, he said, 'If only you had loved her. You didn't love her and you destroyed me.'

He got up and left. I could not get up. Much later, when I

noticed I was crying and went outside, I saw him in the feeble light thrown from the burning tin barrel at the end of the street; he was walking, trailing his black overcoat and merging into the deep darkness of the night.

That was the night Mikail's heart stopped.

RED TORMENT

We were three story characters in our author's mind straining at the leash for our destinies to be written: the Notary, the Young Buck and I. Although we were yet to be written, we had an inkling we would be characters in the same story, and tried to guess what kind of connection our author would establish between us. But there wasn't even a single sentence written to bring the three of us together. That's why we were unable to get close and had to make do with watching one another from afar.

Our story still lacked a definite plot and still kept churning round in our author's head. It wasn't certain what we would be, what we would do, or even whether we would exist at all. We weren't developed enough to form a connection between our existence and what was going through his mind. We knew very little about ourselves. We just wandered aimlessly, heroes as yet unwritten in the supernatural world of story characters. We were on edge, and felt very much alone.

From time to time, our author took notes we thought were related to our story, and which excited us, as he scribbled down the first sentences on sheets of rough paper with his black ink fountain pen. Then he'd crumple it all up and throw it away, thus dragging us into deep obscurity. He couldn't be said to be working on us at any length, or set much of his time to create us. True, he did, from time to time, occupy himself with the Notary, but he usually forgot about the Young Buck and me, and never wrote a single word that would concern me in particular. As he delayed committing me to paper, my hopes about existing rapidly dissolved.

Because I wasn't yet on familiar terms with the characters of other stories, I had focused all my attention on our author. To know that my existence was in his hands gave me an indescribably agreeable feeling. As if there was a divine balance between us. I, and the other story characters, were the ones who gave meaning to our author's life. If he were to create me, I would contribute to his existence. This relationship between the author and the character he wrote about whipped up my desire to exist, exciting me tremendously.

I learnt from the Rag-and-Bone-Man that our author spent a very long time on his stories, that he'd carry the characters in his head for a long time prior to beginning to write, and that there were story characters he'd yet to finish and was still working on. The Rag-and-Bone-Man was the main character of a story that our author had been working on for years. In spite of constant writing, he'd never been able to take his final form, or perhaps deliberately avoided it. I always felt the Rag-and-Bone-Man's comforting presence beside me throughout our story's writing process, when I was at my most desperate.

The Notary, the Young Buck and I had been created separately in our writer's mind. I don't know when and how this started. Once, when we were sitting together, I looked at them both out of the corner of my eye, and had an inkling that we would be in the same story. That's how silent, cold and distant – and even thought-provoking – our beginning was.

What were we going to be? What was going to happen to us? In what kind of existence were we going to blossom? With what kind of personality were we going to enter the minds of our future readers? Which feelings of theirs were we going to touch, and which of their thoughts were we going to ease the birth of? We knew nothing, and the longer our story failed to begin, the more worried we got. Enveloped by the fear we might never exist. Fresh hope filled us every morning when our author went to his table. As our story turned over in his mind we grew excited. Sometimes, just as we were about to appear and just as we were preparing to smile at our existence, our author put down his pen. Then we resumed our long, boring and silent wait.

But this situation didn't last long. Soon after we sensed we were characters in the same story, the Notary grew much more discernible. The Young Buck and I were neglected; not properly described, and without even a couple of words jotted down about us. Our author's indifference brought us closer to each other and distanced us completely from the Notary.

The Notary had now become someone else. The timid man, worried about the game that his uncertain destiny would play on him, was gone; in his place was someone with a cold and arrogant manner, apparently as insensitive as a dead branch. We no longer shared our worries, emotions or expectations. He strutted like an actor who'd landed a glitzy starring role, smiling smugly. A disturbing look had settled in his eyes. He'd also developed insomnia. His huge eyes never closed, shining – even in the deepest dark of the night – like the phosphorus on an accursed watch face that would take us to a tragic annihilation. Even in the moments we slept we felt his presence penetrating our marrow, as a dark shadow.

Our author was always working on him. He'd planned his passions, his foibles, his habits, his strange desires and even the place where he lived. According to our author's notes and the chapters he'd written, the Notary lived alone in an eerie, large, dilapidated house, quite a way from the city, facing a railway line. Every morning he left his house, walked to the station and boarded a train, and he returned by the same route in the evenings. He may not have yet been written completely, but he clearly was set to be an interesting story character. Night and day altered the chemistry of his body. During the day he lived as an ordinary person like everyone else, approved the proper observance of life's infinite details, was overly meticulous in his work while in his dark suit, and became a dedicated part of the established order, one that would remain as such for his whole life. But once the sun disappeared behind the mountains, and the darkness of the night descended upon the earth, a sick, disturbed side claimed his soul, and so the Notary sat in front of the window not blinking an eye until morning, carried away by a profound, sickly loneliness, aflame with longing for emotions he considered forbidden by day.

Even such scant attention had been enough for the other story characters to talk about him. They were whispering to one another, pointing at him, and fussing around him, half admiring, half shy. The Notary too was aware of the situation. That's why he grew increasingly arrogant, scornful of both the Young Buck and me, observing us with eyes full of contempt. So sure he was that he would be the protagonist, that he only deigned to speak to the main characters of the stories already written by our author. He'd altered rapidly and, as the details of his character became clearer, his arrogance increased.

And he didn't stop there. He spread around the conviction in his superiority to such an extent that even talking to a story character virtually became a favour. He began to discriminate between characters and to insult some. The more he did this, the more minor characters flocked around him with flattery, showing more interest than was necessary, and idolising a story character whose existence would be limited to what the author had written.

In the face of all this theatrical interest the Notary grew so grim to appear ridiculous in our supernatural world. Yet ours was an aimless world without rules. In the free zone in our author's mind we lived far from all natural and social laws. The Notary influenced the story characters with his manner and bearing, making it clear he wanted our unconditional surrender. It was plain he'd brought a weird hierarchy to our ungoverned, motley world. The Young Buck, on the other hand, was deeply concerned with the uncertainty of his own destiny. He'd almost lost all interest in his surroundings. Even his sleep was anxious and full of fear. The fear of being non-existent had made him highly irritable. The Rag-and-Bone-Man and I were aware of the dreadfulness of all this, but there was nothing we could do about it.

I got to know the Rag-and-Bone-Man at the time when the Notary was rapidly becoming clearer and our despair increasingly grew. He could have become a permanent fixture in our author's mind. He couldn't remember how many years he had lived in his mind, and how many stories had been started in which he was the main character. He was such a non-written character that he'd virtually become our author's conscience and critic, the inspector of his progress as an author. He'd grown old, and had almost grown into a person in the author's mind.

Throughout the time he remained yet to be written, the Rag-and-Bone-Man had seen so many story characters that to be written or not to be written had lost its importance. He was the only one amongst us who wasn't concerned about existing. I never told him, but I sensed that when our author wrote him the adventure would end, and he'd close his writer's book.

All the story characters were aware of the Rag-and-Bone-Man's importance. They may have flocked to the Notary, but the Rag-and-Bone-Man intimidated them; they made no secret of their deep respect for him.

At the time when the Notary believed with all his heart that he was the greatest story character our author had ever created, he wanted to draw the Rag-and-Bone-Man too into his sphere of influence. But he was flummoxed to see that his forceful manner, that easily manipulated the other story characters, had no effect on the Rag-and-Bone-Man. That's when I felt the Notary had also begun to harbour doubts about his own fate.

One morning, when I was about to give up hope of existing, our author sat down at his desk, and after putting down on paper the Notary-driven plot he'd formed in his mind, he began to write us in. I was in a red dress. The Young Man had a very flashy, bright red car. The Notary was perched like an owl, brooding at the window of his tumbledown house.

The Young Buck overrated this existence and suddenly came to life. Just as I'd once struggled to recognise the Notary, neither did I now recognise the Young Buck. Once he would have preferred non-existence to an existence of just a few lines, but now this person was gone. In his place was a wretched someone who accepted any type of personality just so he could exist in the story. *At last we are being written!* he whooped with joy, overplaying his delight.

Yet I was unhappy because I was going to exist in the same story with the Notary. The feeling that I would be captive in the same story with a person who created a weird hierarchy between us and turned our imaginary world upside down settled into my heart like a profound grief. The Rag-and-Bone-Man was aware of my unhappiness. He'd keep telling me not to lose hope until the final full stop had been placed at the end of the story. He based this on his own experience of the long years of not being written at all, and so tried to placate me But nothing he said in his pleasant voice would help to eradicate the sorrow that had coiled up inside me.

I was sitting in the front seat of the Young Buck's expensive red car. I was in a skimpy red dress, and had painted my lips bright red. Fine black stockings wrapped my long legs. On my feet, high stilettoes; thrown around my shoulders, a fake black fur. I was cheaply smart. I was smoking a cigarette. The Young Buck's lust for me exuded out of his skin.

It was very late at night. The houses were growing sparser, their lights long since gone out, and the people of the city had abandoned themselves to the embrace of a tired sleep. The car lapped up the tarmac road a few metres above a railway line. We'd yet to reach the Notary's house that resembled a big black eye in a big, derelict garden. The Young Buck's high spirits were obvious. He was drunk, just as our author wanted. He opened the window and yelled with delight as he pressed down on the accelerator.

Now I knew for certain we were serving the Notary's story. We existed as unremarkable story characters. We'd be forgotten in just one reading, doomed to struggle to find a place in one of the most worthless corners of our supernatural world and so remain unexceptional.

I, too, was drunk. I'd opened the window. From time to time I put out my bare arm into the gently falling snow, trying to cool my skin that burnt like fire. The Young Buck was driving the car with one hand, with the other, he'd pulled my skirt up and started to stroke my leg. I pushed his hand away; he took no notice. His hands grew increasingly more boorish and indicated his delight in the part he was given. This time I pushed his hand away firmly, telling him not to touch me. He slapped me and shouted 'Whore!' I hit him back. Suddenly we were fighting. While I was trying to hit him he was saying he'd paid me in advance and he could do what he liked; grabbing my hair, he was banging my head against the car window, then letting go and squeezing my throat, or slapping me repeatedly.

I was hurting. I was trying to hold his powerful hand, tense with anger, in order to escape the slaps raining down on my face, but could not succeed. The car slowed down briefly when he took his foot of the accelerator; I opened the door and threw myself out. I rolled a few metres down to the railway line. I collapsed on the rails.

As the warmth of the blood flowing from my nose spread over my face, I heard the sharp whistle of a train. I wanted to get up, but couldn't. The train rushed round the bend, speeding toward me, its gigantic headlights instantly lighting up the immediate surroundings. I shut my eyes tight and cursed my author. The train sped towards me and I was cast as an unlucky, short-lived story character who'd taste this death at every reading.

The sound of the whistle died away and then was heard no longer. I opened my eyes, confused. The harsh lights had vanished, and the place had fallen into pitch darkness. The train hadn't left my body behind it; it had passed by on the other side of the two-way track. I struggled up, sensing my story had actually now begun. The Notary's unlit house seemed to be calling me, a huge silhouette in the darkness of the night. I began to walk towards my destiny in tired, distraught steps.

My nose was still bleeding. My hair was a mess, my fur was caught on the brambles, and my patent leather shoes had flown off my feet. I was freezing. Covering my naked bosom with my lacerated, bare arms, I entered the Notary's derelict garden and hammered on the iron door of the house. My author had written he'd seen everything and was now waiting for me. The Notary of the phosphorous eyes opened the door. I fainted in his skinny, bony arms. When I came round in a huge bed in the middle of a large room, at that very short moment between day and night, I saw the Notary who'd stroked my ankles all night long taking his dark suit from the wardrobe in preparation for the day.

I hadn't died, but had become the Notary's prisoner. This was worse than death. I wasn't happy with my existence. But what really undid me was not this, but the Young Buck's excessive satisfaction. Gone was the sensitive, innocent young man, whose childish features gave one an irresistible urge to stroke them. He was trying to ingratiate himself with the Notary and could barely contain his joy. I was utterly confused. We weren't actually in this story. We weren't instrumental in telling anything. I was a common whore, and he was a wretched young man. We were the means for the Notary's existence. The Young Buck didn't care about any of this. He was guffawing as he told other story characters how he slapped me, and what he felt when he was stroking my legs. He'd become so contemptible that he didn't refrain from paying compliments to the Notary – whom he'd hated before he came into being – telling him he was the greatest story character of all time. And the Notary in turn indulged the Young Buck, virtually rewarding him with smiles.

But something totally unexpected happened one night. The Rag-and-Bone-Man came over and said our author just couldn't get to sleep. Sure enough: our author was tossing and turning in his bed. I looked at the Young Buck. Exhausted with delight, he was sound sleep, an idiotic expression on his face. But our author's restlessness had attracted the Notary's attention. Our eyes met. A transparent shadow of fear shaded his ever-open eyes. At long last our author got up, sat down at his desk and settled down to work.

At the end of a fevered bout of work of several weeks, the Notary and the Young Buck disappeared. The Notary was bewildered, devastated. He couldn't believe he'd been sacrificed. And the Young Buck was left dumbstruck, a frozen smile on his lips, unable to understand what had happened. In time they faded, and vanished altogether when the last piece of paper was thrown away.

This incident very much surprised the other story characters too. It actually shook them all. And then they began to talk about how the Notary could have impressed them all so much; they confessed to their shame of the state into which they had fallen in their efforts to please him. The colourful, jubilant world of story characters slowly began to regain its former glory.

I was the one who remained from that unfinished story. I lived for a long period in our author's mind as a cheap-looking woman in a red dress with red lipstick. Then one morning our author began my story. I came out of a tavern with a story character I'd never seen before. Again it was late at night. We got into the sad-eyed. Timid Young Buck's wreck of a car, and began to drive along the same coastal road. We were both drunk. It was I who'd seduced him.

We were going to a summerhouse, where I was going to take off my fake black fur, my black silk stockings, my patent leather shoes and red dress, to introduce this shy sensitive young man to that feeling called lust. As the car travelled towards the point where I'd rolled down to the tracks, the Timid Young Man touched my legs with nervous and inexperienced fingers. Everything was as our author had written. The fickle prostitute past her prime that I was, I changed my mind about sleeping with this young man. All of a sudden, I pushed his hand away and began to insult him. I said, just because he'd paid me, he couldn't do whatever he wanted to me. He was astonished, awkward. He was sorry, had already stopped touching me, but this time I was the one written as a different character. I was loathsome and drunk. I was swearing at him and bawling my eyes out.

I opened the window and began to scream. The lights came on in some of the houses lining the road. The Timid Young Man was trying to calm me down. He began to beg me to be quiet; I was not quiet. My screams pierced the night. As he tried to close my mouth with his hand, the door of the old car suddenly opened and I rolled down to the same railway track, from the same place. Again the same train appeared. Its headlights illuminated the surroundings like daylight.

The train passed by on the track next to me. Again blood was seeping from my nose. I got up and walked towards the sea. I leant against a tree. I was drunk and despondent. Suddenly, I heard the young man's screams. He thought I'd been run over by the train, and was struggling down the slope.

He looked like he'd gone berserk as he sank onto the railway track. 'Where are you?' he shouted several times. He was frightened and wretched. All of a sudden, a train appeared, coming in the opposite direction. The sharp whistle diffused towards the sea. The headlights lit up the surroundings. I heard the echo of his scream and his body being torn apart. A pain pierced my heart just then. I became acquainted with a bright red torment.

Thus we came into being in the world of story characters. The romantic, gentle-eyed Timid Young Man always said I was a good story friend. I replied, 'If only our author had also written your fiancée!' If our author had written his story differently... but he was to be married the following day. All he wanted was to spend his last bachelor night with me.

www.ingramcontent.com/pod-product-compliance
Lightning Source LLC
Chambersburg PA
CBHW020341260626
47156CB00004B/1632